PROPERTIES OF LOVE

A Sweet Romance

Billionaire's Bet

Book 3

A.B. PROEBSTEL

ISBN-13: 978-1-946292-36-0

ISBN-10: 1-946292-36-2

Printed in the United States of America

First Printing, 2020

Second Printing, 2022

Third Printing, 2023

Website: https://geni.us/LOA-Home
BookBub: https://geni.us/BBFollow
Goodreads: www.goodreads.com/aproebstel
Facebook: https://geni.us/FB-LOA
X: https://geni.us/Amy-T
Instagram: www.instagram.com/amyproebstel

Books in the Billionaire's Bet Series

Book Zero: A Billionaire's Patent for Love

Book One: A Cowboy's Recipe for Romance

Book Two: Loving Texas Tea

Book Three: Properties of Love

Book Four: Plane Love

Book Five: Capitalizing on Love

Book Six: An Unleashed Love

Book Seven: Ether of Love

DEDICATION

First of all, this book is dedicated to my friends and family. Your support in helping me carve out time to write and your encouragement to keep me going even when life got in the way, has been utterly amazing. I've been so inspired by your thoughtfulness and I hope it shows in my writing.

Secondly, to the readers of this series, I greatly appreciate all of your kind words, amazing reviews, and support along the way. None of this would be possible without your enthusiasm for the characters and their stories.

CHAPTER 1

MICHAEL

Impatience gnawed at Michael like a restless tiger as he stood in the Title company, waiting to get his hands on the all-important land deed documents. He tapped his foot impatiently, but then his gaze fell on the stunning woman working at the desk across from him. Well, that certainly made the wait more tolerable.

When his phone buzzed in his pocket, he was ready to growl in frustration, but his friend's name on the caller ID saved him from any outbursts. Turning away from the captivating woman, Michael leaned against the well-worn counter, phone pressed to his ear.

"They have no idea what's happening in their neighborhood," Michael chuckled, feeling like he was about to spill some top-secret heist. "I've been snapping up these properties at one-tenth of the value I'll have by this time next year."

His friend on the other end was probably shaking his head in disbelief at Michael's lucky streak. Little did he know the hours of research and strategic planning Michael had put into this game. Oh, it was all about to pay off big time.

Michael chuckled at his personal coup, once again lining his ultra-wealthy pockets with unsuspecting people's properties. He didn't see the shabby office around him; instead, he focused on the plans for the construction of a massive mall complex.

His careful research and donations in the right places allowed him the knowledge to always show up in the right place at the right time. He let people believe in his incredible luck, but he knew all of the hours of reading and listening that went into his particular kind of success. So much rode on him making a name for himself.

For years, he had been under his father's watchful eye, working in the family business. But Michael wanted to prove himself, to carve out his own legacy. So, he took a leap of faith, and now he was the king of his real estate empire.

But what amused him the most was how people underestimated him just because he looked young for his twenty-seven years They thought they had the upper hand, and Michael loved watching their smug faces turn to disbelief when he outsmarted them at every turn. He was a real estate ninja, stealthily maneuvering through contracts and negotiations.

But they learned. The tiger was on the prowl, and he was about to make another killing in the real estate jungle. And when he walked away with deals others thought were impossible, he would do it with finesse and class, never once gloating. After all, what's a victory without a little mystery and style?

Despite his privileged upbringing in his father's billion-dollar investment company, family life had been anything but happy. His parents' constant discord drove him away from their opulent mansion and into the arms of his loving grandmother.

Suddenly, the air around him filled with a tantalizing scent of vanilla, signaling the approach of someone he knew all too well. Just as expected, a thick manila envelope landed on the countertop behind him. With a slick smile, Michael swiftly ended his phone call and turned around to face the source of the delightful fragrance.

Jocelyn.

Her shoulder-length blonde hair framed her captivating doe eyes, and Michael couldn't help but admire her beauty.

Despite his cheeky demeanor, he felt genuine gratitude for her speedy service. However, the playful glint in his eyes clashed with her stern expression.

"Thanks, Josie. I appreciate the speedy service, as always," he said with a smirk, purposely using the nickname he knew annoyed her.

"It's Jocelyn, Mr. Cavanaugh, but whatever," she retorted, rolling her eyes before making a swift exit.

Her sassy departure only amused him further, and he couldn't help but admire her from behind as she walked away. He loved riling her; she made it so easy.

Maybe he had been going about it all wrong with her. Perhaps instead of riling her up, he should try a different approach. He found himself contemplating the idea of asking her out.

After his last relationship fizzled out a couple of months ago, he had kept to himself, focusing on work and more important pursuits. But just the thought of Jocelyn's full lips against his brought a mischievous glimmer to his eyes. Yes, maybe it was time to soften up the prickly little Jocelyn and see where that might lead. After all, what's life without a little excitement and a lot of charm?

With the hefty packet in hand, Michael couldn't help but admire Jocelyn's meticulous work. Her attention to detail impressed him more than she could ever imagine, and it was the reason he almost exclusively used this shabby, old title company for his business. Loose ends and delays were not something he could tolerate. Any hiccup could jeopardize a deal, and that was simply unacceptable in his world.

Feeling the documents safely tucked under his arm, he had more than business on his mind as he strode out of the bustling office into the sultry heat of the Georgian sun. The idea of winning over Josie occupied his thoughts, and he couldn't help but devise a charming plan.

He paid no attention to the beauty of the flowering hibiscus right in front of his car. If someone dared to ask him about the scenery, they would have received a blank stare. Scenery? Who had time for that? He had deals to close and ventures to conquer.

In the scorching heat, he refused to loosen his tie. Maintaining the image of a cool and composed businessman was crucial, after all. Luckily, he had snagged the prime parking spot near the entrance, allowing him to reach his sleek Mercedes AMG with ease. As he settled into the luxurious leather seat, he couldn't escape the heat, even with the window cracked open.

The car's interior felt like an oven, and he half-jokingly wondered if he could bake cookies on the dashboard. Despite the sweltering heat, he kept his focus on his next task, his mind buzzing with ideas and strategies.

Tossing the paperwork onto the passenger seat, Michael started the engine with a smooth gesture. The vents immediately blasted hot air into his face, but he knew relief was on the way as the AC kicked in.

With the tunes blaring from the radio, he sped out of the parking lot, squeezing his car into a tight space between two vehicles, earning a honk from the impatient driver behind him. Crazy drivers couldn't deter him; he had places to be and promises to keep.

With five minutes to spare, he pulled into his reserved parking space. As Georgia's most eligible bachelor, he was used to the attention from women, single or married, everywhere he went, but he doggedly ignored the staff's stares. His past experiences had taught him to keep his guard up, protecting himself from getting hurt again.

Navigating through the bright and colorful hallways, he hardly noticed the colorful paintings on the walls, his mind preoccupied with more pressing matters. Finally, he reached the room that held someone dearer to him than anything else in the world. A deep breath steadied him as he prepared for the encounter.

With a light tap on the six-panel wooden door, he turned the shiny, brass handle to let himself in, fully expecting to see a familiar smile greeting him.

But as he entered, he was taken aback. Instead of his grandma, a stranger occupied the room. "Who are you?" Michael blurted out, pushing his way inside to find his beloved grandmother.

His mind spun with dreadful scenarios in the absence of his grandma, none of them offering any comfort. His heart raced like a runaway train, and his eyes darted around the room in panic. Everything in his grandma's room remained undisturbed—the dressers, coffee table, and chairs—yet she was nowhere to be seen.

"Come sit down, Michael. Let me explain why I'm here today," the man said without rising or even introducing himself.

Already suspicious, Michael didn't trust the stranger, resenting the fact that he knew his name without any proper introduction. The man exuded self-assurance, just like his father, and it put him on edge.

Hating to be caught off guard, Michael needed all the facts before making any decisions—this felt like a cold business transaction, and he wanted no part of it, especially if it meant his grandma had passed away.

"I'll stand," Michael replied curtly, feeling the uncomfortable trickle of sweat down his back. His main concern was his grandma's whereabouts, and he demanded, "Where's Evelyn?"

"I'm right here, Mikey. Come help me to my bed." A frail, trembling voice emanated from the doorway leading to the private bathroom. Michael's heart clenched as he saw his grandma's fragile figure, ravaged by the relentless grasp of Parkinson's disease.

Without hesitation, Michael hurried to her side, gently enveloping her in his embrace. Using his height and strength, he supported her, realizing how much more weight she had lost. Concern and fear flooded him as he felt the prominence of her bones through the rich silk fabric of her dressing robe.

Michael couldn't bear to see his grandma's frailty, so he carefully positioned her in the middle of the bed, gently fluffing the pillows behind her delicate frame. He feared that even his touch might be too much for her weakened state.

Biting his bottom lip to suppress his emotions, he stepped back and turned his attention to the stranger in the room. He needed to focus on this man's business to distract himself from the overwhelming worry.

Evelyn arranged the covers just as she liked them and she patted the edge of the bed. Her once strong voice now barely a whisper said, "Mikey, sit next to me and listen to what Mr. Nitro has to say."

Mr. Nitro? What kind of name was that? It sounded phony, just like the smile plastered on the man's pudgy face. Before following his grandma's instruction, Michael muttered, "Mr. Nitro, if that's your real name," and then boldly asked, "Why are you here?"

"Be nice, Mikey. Kevin is my attorney, and he has been for many years," Evelyn chided, her trembling hand reaching for his thigh.

Disliking the feel of her tremors, Michael pressed his hand down gently over hers, trying to offer some comfort. The feeble strength of her hold only made him feel more helpless. No amount of money could fix the person he loved most in the world. He nodded reluctantly, shifting his gaze back to the unwanted guest.

"I'm here at your grandmother's behest," Kevin said, seeking Evelyn's approval before continuing. Satisfied with her nod, he continued, "It seems Ms. Evelyn has received the results of her latest tests and only has about six months left to live."

His jaw clenched. He despised the fact that this man had such news about his grandma, news that he hadn't been made aware of before.

Tension gripped Michael as he tried to keep his fingers relaxed, not wanting to hurt his grandma with his own fear. He vehemently shook his head in denial, refusing to accept the harsh truth. "I don't believe you. We're going to have them redo the tests."

Turning to his grandma, desperation in his eyes, he hoped she would contradict the attorney's words. But her sad gaze confirmed the dreadful news. "If this place can't take care of your needs properly, then we'll move you to a better facility. Money's no object. I'll start making phone calls right now."

His hand instinctively reached for his phone in his front pocket, but her next words halted him in his tracks.

"You'll do nothing of the kind, Michael."

She only called him by his given name when he was in trouble.

Feeling chastised and embarrassed in front of a stranger, Michael nodded mutely, biting back the sharp retort he wanted to make. "State your business, Mr. Nitro, so that I can have some private time with my grandma." More than ever, he wanted to have these precious moments alone with the woman who had practically raised him.

"Evelyn wanted me to advise you about a change she has made in her Will," Kevin started, leaning forward to pull out a stack of papers from his briefcase.

"Discussing her Will while she's here with us is unnecessary and insensitive. The last thing she needs is you drumming up more billable hours with unnecessary house calls," Michael retorted sharply, his mind racing with worry for his grandma. The Will was the last thing on his mind; he couldn't bear the thought of losing her.

Finding the section he wanted to discuss in the document, Kevin continued as if Michael hadn't interrupted. He cleared his throat and began reading, "To my grandson, Michael Theodore Cavanaugh, I bequeath the family farm of 30,000 acres of land, 17 outbuildings, and the main homestead, including all of the personal items found in the home and on the property in its entirety.

"However, because this is a family farm, it is only proper that Michael inherit it with his own family, to wit, his wife and/or children of his own issue.

"If, at the time of my death, Michael is unmarried, then the land will revert to the county to be made a proper wildlife refuge held in trust for all time. All of the bank accounts associated with this property, valued as of this date at $2.78 billion dollars, will also be held in trust for the maintenance of the land as a wildlife refuge."

As the words sank into Michael's numb brain, anger surged within him at the injustice of this new clause in the Will. Throughout his life, his grandma had promised him the farm, knowing it had been the only sanctuary he'd known during his troubled childhood.

"I can't believe this, Grandma! You know how I feel about marriage," Michael protested vehemently, his voice tinged with frustration.

Michael's heart pounded with indignation. He had no intention of getting married just to secure the farm, but he couldn't bear the thought of losing the place he called home to strangers. He needed time to think, to find a solution, and to fight for what he believed was rightfully his.

"Yes, Mikey. I've heard your grumblings about marriage more times than I care to count," his grandma replied calmly. "But it's time for you to set aside your hurt and pride and let someone into your heart. The right woman will make you into the man you were always meant to be."

Her words stung him to the core, reopening wounds he thought had healed long ago. Fear and uncertainty crept into his voice as he asked, "Aren't you proud of me the way I am?"

Feeling doubly betrayed, Michael couldn't believe his beloved grandma would speak to him like this. Maybe the disease was already affecting her mental capacities, and it filled him with anger and desperation. Dementia was one of the final symptoms to develop in cases such as hers. He was prepared to fight this new addendum, even if it meant declaring her with diminished capacity.

"Yes, Mikey, you've always been the perfect grandson," she replied, her tone unwavering. "And before you get any ideas that I'm getting soft in the head, I know exactly what I'm doing. I want to ensure you're taken care of before I meet my maker. Besides, it's high time you start thinking about making me a great-grandma, just in case I decide to kick this

Parkinson's in the butt." Evelyn reached over with her free hand and patted the back of Michael's hand where he still held onto her.

A fresh wave of guilt washed over him as she seemed to read his thoughts. How could he refuse her plea? If the idea of him getting married and having children could give her hope and incentive to live, then he'd have to put aside his reservations and give marriage a try. But the memory of his failed relationships, especially his last one with Angelica, made him hesitant.

His track record was pretty bad. He had no idea how to find the perfect partner.

Reluctantly, Michael realized he had no choice but to appease his grandma's wishes. The thought of losing the family farm to the Public Lands Division made his blood boil and fueled his determination to find a solution, even if it meant stepping into a world of uncertainty and taking another chance on love.

Probably just what his grandma had in mind when she put in the provision.

His grandma's underhanded tactic impressed and frustrated him simultaneously. He couldn't deny the guilt weighing on him as her condition loomed in his mind.

"I don't even know where to start," Michael lamented under his breath, the weight of the responsibility heavy on his shoulders.

To his surprise, his grandma heard him. "Start closest to home. You know, people you work with. Surely there're some good girls who understand real estate. As soon as you open your eyes, you'll start to notice how the girls look at you when you walk past. It's time you got your head out of your bank account and started listening to your heart's call for love."

Embarrassment washed over him again, knowing that the looks he received were often connected to his wealth, not his character. He didn't want a relationship built on material possessions; his failed experience with Angelica had taught him that. It made him feel dirty.

He struggled to keep his composure, resisting the urge to roll his eyes at her advice. His heart was just fine the way it was, unattached and free from complications. He had no intention of being bossed around or giving up his independence. As far as he was concerned, his life was already perfect – no attachments, no distractions, and most importantly, no disappointments.

However, the gravity of his grandma's request couldn't be ignored. He would do anything to make her happy, but the task ahead seemed monumental.

Forgetting entirely about the harbinger of bad news sitting across the room from him, Michael's mind raced through this latest task.

Determined to face it like a business transaction, he realized he had six months to find the perfect bride and secure the family farm. Maybe if he viewed it from a pragmatic standpoint, it would give his grandma the will to live even longer. After all, she never mentioned anything about love or longevity in her demand.

CHAPTER 2
JOCELYN

Jocelyn knew watching the clock would only make the end of the day take forever to roll around. When five o'clock struck, she had already turned her computer off, and her purse looped over her arm. Now, she simply had to get past her boss's office without him calling her in to 'talk' for the next half of an hour.

Nothing on Earth could convince her to take any interest in her boss. He obviously harbored a fascination with her bordering on unprofessional, even to the extent of sexual harassment. If she felt so inclined, she had ample cause to pursue a claim with human resources.

Yet, she knew she wouldn't say anything. She needed this job to pay for a new car. Every spare penny got squirreled away into an account, waiting for the day she had enough to get the car she'd pined over for the past two years. A Toyota Prius. Nothing fancy, nothing to write home about, but it was affordable and economical on gas, which she desperately needed.

Ever since her parents had literally had to sell the farm, her drive out to their condominium two cities over to the west had all but bankrupted her with the fuel consumption costs. Guilt and love prevented her from ever complaining. Also, worry over her father's health ensured she never missed a weekend visit with them.

Her mom insisted he was taking things easy, but Jocelyn believed in her core that the spare time ate at her father's soul. He'd worked hard to maintain the family farm all of his life, waking up before the sun to get all his chores done before the scorching heat sent him scurrying for a reprieve in the shade of a tree by the creek.

No, her father definitely needed a hobby. He needed something to get his mind off how badly the real estate agent had taken advantage of their ignorance when they sold the farm. Even though Jocelyn had been in college at the time of the sale, she felt responsible for not checking in to see whether or not the price had been fair.

That one moment in time had changed all of their lives. Even now, Jocelyn could feel her rage building that her parents didn't have the comfy retirement nest egg they had counted on. She hated how they'd been forced to live in a crappy housing complex in an iffy part of their city simply to extend their meager savings. And as for herself, she gave up her dream of becoming a vet tech to go into the business side of real estate.

Her original idea of becoming a real estate agent to help protect other old couples from getting taken advantage of certainly hadn't panned out. After only three college courses, she realized she hated dealing with disappointing people by telling them the actual value of their place or that they'd have to spend money to get the price they wanted. Nope, that hadn't been the path for her.

Instead, she'd gone to work for the United Title Company of the South. The old, worn building had been the last stop on her employment search. Even during her interview, she'd had a bad feeling about Mr. Bandy, who'd be her boss, but she needed the job to pay for her student loans and keep her from losing the tiny apartment she'd managed to find nearby.

This job ticked all of her financial boxes. As an added benefit, she educated herself about the properties she had to research. Research thrilled her more than she cared to admit to casual strangers since most people tended to find it terrible to contemplate and boring to discuss.

Unfortunately, her talents only seemed to help people like the ones who had swindled her parents. People like Michael Cavanaugh. She felt her lip curling in distaste, even thinking about him and his over-the-top ego.

Nearing Mr. Bandy's door, she could hear him speaking on the phone. Taking a calculated risk, she pretended to look through her purse, keeping her face averted from the opening as she skipped past the doorway. This way, if he decided to wave at her to get her attention, she could honestly say she hadn't seen it.

The employee door snapped shut behind her, sealing off the cold air inside, which always seemed directly aimed at wherever she sat, sinking deep into her bones until she thought she might freeze solid. The sultry heat of the lowering sun settled across her like a welcoming shawl. Drawing in a deep breath of the hot, lemon-scented air, she felt the tension melt away from her. Work always made her tense, which probably didn't help the ulcers she started experiencing.

With a welcoming sigh of relief, not only from her escape from work but from the dreaded air-conditioning, she paused to appreciate the heat of the day beginning to thaw her ice-cold fingers. She strode across the small parking lot reserved for employees with a surreptitious glance to check her surroundings.

Her mind reveled in the stark contrasts ahead of her. The asphalt shimmered with heat, but the proud magnolia tree spread her thick branches of green leaves and huge, bright, creamy blossoms outward to shade several cars in the lot.

She could easily imagine a time when this tree stood alone in an empty field, giving a fragrant refuge to a child who could escape into a world of dreams and possibility. She'd gladly trade the mess the tree left on her beat-up, silver Honda Civic for the lovely scent and the coolness underneath.

The smile curving her lips from her fanciful imaginings slightly dimmed when she realized Mr. Bandy parked his fancy BMW beside her car. The two vehicles, side-by-side, further showed the contrast in her economic situation compared to his. Yet, she didn't dwell on her physical possessions since this car merely allowed her more accessible transportation. It didn't have to be pretty.

Her luck continued to hold out as the driver's side door actually opened. At least today, she wouldn't have to crawl across the front from the passenger's side, which started to become a regular occurrence.

Still, the hinges protested as she cracked open the door just far enough to squeeze herself in, sarcastically thanking Mr. Bandy for parking so close to the line to force her to stretch in strange contortions to keep from hitting his car with her door.

Granted, he probably assumed she'd have to get in from the passenger side, as he often saw her do in the past, much to her intense embarrassment. If Mr. Bandy really wanted to be helpful, he should consider giving her a raise so she could get the new car sooner. Maybe, he just enjoyed watching her struggle. Or even worse, perhaps he enjoyed catching glimpses of her chest or legs should she happen to be wearing a scooped neckline or pencil skirt that day. She couldn't dwell on that thought; it just grossed her out.

With goosebumps raised all over her arms, she luxuriated in the heated interior of her car. Slipping off her low heels, she wriggled her feet into the sneakers she used for driving and carefully laced them up. One could never be too careful while driving.

The last thing Jocelyn needed was for her pump's heel to get caught in the hole in the floor mat just when she needed to brake or something just as dire. She'd gladly forego fashion for safety any day.

Jocelyn hoped her luck stayed strong and the car would decide to start on the first try. Strangely, it felt as though the car found out about the saved money, increasingly developing irritating issues. So far, she managed to handle them herself, like replacing the windshield wiper, which decided to fly off as she drove down the highway in the pouring rain. And she simply ignored the funny little light flickering on the panel, which didn't mean anything to her.

The mechanics didn't interest her; she only wanted reliable transportation. Today, Blondie, the name she gave her car almost ten years prior, decided to behave. The engine sputtered to life on the first try, and hot air blew into her face from the vents.

Out of habit, she pushed the vent aside while rolling down the window with the old-fashioned crank—no power windows for this girl. No dreaded air-conditioning either, unless driving faster counted.

Shifting the car into reverse, she let out the clutch as quickly as ever, but the vehicle still lurched as if she were a novice driver. Ignoring Blondie's quirks, she waited and waited at the curb, only entering the traffic flow when a kind, old lady waved her to go. Not that they got very far, very fast, in the stop-and-go traffic. Once again, she gave thanks for the short commute to her small apartment where only her cat, Meow Meow, cared if she arrived safely.

The song's lyrics playing on the tinny-sounding radio reminded her of her mother's not-so-subtle hints about bringing a boyfriend home for Thanksgiving, even though it was a solid six months away. No amount of talking could convince her mother that no man interested her enough to date, let alone someone she would consider letting her parents grill. She stopped bringing boys home ever since that dreaded prom night.

While she didn't plan to spend the rest of her life alone, she also wouldn't lower her standards just for the sake of having some guy hanging around. Besides, she didn't need someone else to take care of; her cat's medical issues took enough of her free time.

Groaning with dismay, she realized her commute time had just doubled when she remembered she needed to stop by Piggly Wiggly's to get more cat food before going home. Although Meow Meow didn't seem to mind the can of tuna she got the night before, Jocelyn hated the fishy breath wafting across her face all night long as she shared her pillow. Besides, the man she brought home would be allergic to her favorite feline with her luck.

Another reason she didn't need a man; she liked sharing her bed with the cat. At least the cat didn't snore; well, she did start the terrible habit of clawing her hair in the morning and licking her scalp to wake her up at alarmingly early times. No man needed to see her morning hair literally looking like something the cat dragged in.

Okay, so maybe the cat wasn't that perfect a roommate. But at least she didn't demand too much of her time. In fact, she often needed to search for the feline, usually found under the bed, while she waited for her to come home. At least the cat kept the dust bunnies under control as they provided endless hours of entertainment.

Fine, she admitted it to herself; her life was rather pathetic. She didn't want to become the crazy cat lady, only leaving the house to buy cat food and litter. In fact, she made sure never to have any pet hair on her clothing because that seemed like another inevitable symptom of becoming a hermit.

She didn't have the time or inclination to find someone who would fit into her life. Just hearing the horror stories of people using online dating sites or those other dreaded dating apps made her skin crawl. No, she didn't want to be the next news headline story about another girl gone missing after using such drastic measures to find the perfect man who probably didn't exist. He remained the veritable unicorn.

Maybe she'd take up going to church again. Now that she had settled into her apartment, she had the time. For several days, this thought kept coming back to her. Yesterday, she even did a quick search online to get the sermon schedules. She simply needed to get herself together enough on the weekend actually to want to leave the house.

The traffic light turned green in front of her. As if on autopilot, she pressed the gas pedal, blindly following the car ahead of her into the intersection. With the driveway for the grocery store in sight, she never saw the car pull away from the crossroad to turn into her lane.

Sounds of metal screeching, glass shattering, and plastic popping seemed to fill her mind as the impact jarred her into a strange sense of awareness. Time seemed to crawl into slow motion as her car moved into the next lane with the crash force. Snippets of clarity impressed her mind, like the surprised expressions on the passengers' faces in the car next to her just before their vehicles collided.

Only seconds passed, but the silence that followed the onslaught of noise seemed out of place. Strangely enough, her mind focused on the song that started playing from her car's radio right after all went still; it was a new song by Becky Easton about a red, high-heeled shoe being left behind. Somehow, that seemed fitting for this scenario of destruction.

Looking down, her whitened knuckles clutched the steering wheel as if her life depended on that continued contact. Maybe it did. Hot tears rolling down her cheeks triggered the trembling, which crawled through her whole body. When did she start crying? She allowed her body to have the minor release it seemed so desperate to take.

With fresh adrenaline coursing through her veins, she felt an urgent need to get moving, to get out of her car, if only to check on the other people involved. After taking quick stock of herself, she pried one hand away from the useless steering wheel to pull on the door latch.

A surge of panic percolated through her as the door remained unmovable. Pushing harder, getting her shoulder into the movement to add more force, she stared stupidly down at her hand to make sure she was doing it right. Nothing. The door wouldn't budge.

A tapping sounded on the passenger window, which somehow managed to stay intact, even though the back one blew out. Her gaze cut across the car's interior to see a man staring back at her with fear in his eyes. She faintly heard him ask, "Are you okay?"

Nodding, she replied, "My door won't open."

The man opened the passenger door without any difficulty. Leaning in, he spoke slowly, acting as if she were a frightened animal that needed to be coaxed to cooperate. "Of course, it won't open; there's a car pinning it shut. Come across this way, Jocelyn. I'll help you."

Dumbly, she twisted to look back to the door, verifying the man's assessment of the jam. How did she miss seeing the other car? This whole situation felt like a dream, where things simply appeared out of thin air.

She tried to scoot across the center console – a task she performed more times than any other adult, but something still immobilized her. "I can't move!" she cried out, panic setting in.

"It's okay; you need to unfasten your seatbelt first." Without invitation, he reached across the passenger seat to push the little release button on the belt. "Let me help you."

Instantly, Jocelyn felt stupid. Why couldn't she keep herself together? With another burst of adrenaline, she whipped the belt off her shoulder, grabbed her purse from the floorboard although she had left it in the passenger seat, and crawled across the cabin in the most unladylike fashion. As promised, the man's hand remained steady as he held onto hers while she found her footing on the blessedly solid pavement.

The man shifted her to the side before diving back into her car. She stared uncomprehendingly but didn't say anything as she stood there like a Grecian statue, pale and stiff. Another picture perfectly formed in her mind as she inappropriately ogled his posterior while he rummaged inside her vehicle.

"You don't want to forget these," he said as he straightened up, holding out her ring of keys.

"Oh, thank you!" Jocelyn gushed, automatically holding out her hand. Her gaze traveled up from his hand to his well-tailored suit covering his beautifully trim, muscular chest, finally coming to rest squarely on the face of the man who regularly drove her insane. "Michael Cavanaugh? What are you doing here?"

With a grim smile, he pointed behind Jocelyn and said, "Exhibit A."

Jocelyn turned her head to see his once-immaculate car in a crumpled heap beside hers. Turning back to him, she demanded, "You did this?"

CHAPTER 3

MICHAEL

"It certainly wasn't on purpose," Michael defended himself. "Are you okay?"

Jocelyn nodded, but she looked dazed and confused.

With his typical take-charge attitude, he grabbed her shoulders and spoke clearly as if to a dull-witted child, "Stay put while I check on the people whose car you hit." He saw some color begin to return to her pale cheeks at the mention of other people involved. Turning away, he thought, out of all the people in the world, how had he managed to hit her car?

After getting the other people situated, Michael pulled out his phone and began making calls. In no time at all, he had contacted his personal assistant, who then took care of calling the police, tow trucks, a fire crew, an ambulance, just for good measure, and several rental cars.

He didn't need this distraction right now. Although, if he were being honest with himself, his distraction had caused this mess to begin with. If he hadn't been so worried about his grandma's health and her ultimatum, he would have noticed his light had been red.

Finishing the call, he pocketed his phone before returning to where Jocelyn had moved onto the sidewalk staring at the scene with a blank, glazed expression. He worried she'd actually hit her head and needed medical attention after all. The idea that he might have killed her caused his heart to clench uncomfortably. She deserved better, much better.

Maybe fate had put her in his path on purpose, he suddenly thought. Instantly, he felt foolish for such a girly, romantic thought. While his grandma may have planted the idea in his head, only he could dwell on it. And he refused to allow himself to be suckered into something as foolish as a rash relationship.

Relationship? Why had his mind gone there? Michael's hands reached up to touch his own skull to see if maybe he'd managed to concuss himself with the strangeness of his train of thought.

Needing to act casual about the whole affair, he changed the assessing motion to his hands simply running through his hair, tousling the ends in his distraction. Jocelyn needed his focus, he reminded himself. Stepping up onto the curb, he stopped in front of her frail-looking form, suddenly wishing he could take her into his arms to comfort them both.

"Help is on its way. Thank goodness it's not raining." Michael clamped his mouth shut before anything more inane could burst from his lips.

"Yes, rain would make this worse," Jocelyn agreed, although her flat voice clearly showed her mind dwelled on something else entirely. She bit her bottom lip, and tears continued to drop from her eyes.

Without thinking, Michael reached up and caught one of the tears on the tip of his index finger. He'd never seen a woman cry silently before, yet it somehow made it worse than if she'd screamed and raged at him. "Jocelyn, are you sure you're okay?"

As if his kind words triggered the flood gates to open, she seemed to crumple in on herself. The volume of tears increased, and she started to mumble incoherently. Michael leaned in closer, desperate to make things right with her. Something about a woman named Blondie seemed to trouble her the most.

"Jocelyn, was there someone in the car with you?" he asked, his eyes raking over the accident scene for a body somehow unnoticed before. When she didn't answer right away, he took hold of her shoulders and gave her a small shake, her head rolling slightly as if she still didn't have complete control of her body yet. "Jocelyn! Answer me! Was someone with you?"

"With me?" she asked, her voice small. Her eyes seemed to focus on him finally, and her shoulders stiffened under his touch. "What're you talking about?"

"You were worried about Blondie. Was she with you?"

"Blondie? Of course she was with me! How else do you think we got into this mess?"

Michael's panic threatened to overtake his good sense as her angry words seemed at odds with her distraction. If Blondie were hurt, surely she'd be trying to find her, but she remained rooted to the concrete. Needing to take action, Michael pressed, "Jocelyn, where's Blondie?"

His gaze followed her pointing finger toward the crash site. Nothing had changed since the last time he'd looked. Had she become delirious? Something didn't add up. His wits must have been dulled since it took him another full minute before he realized she must have been talking about her car.

Suppressing a chuckle, he asked, "Did you name your car Blondie?"

"Yes. And now she's gone." A fresh wave of tears coursed down her cheeks as her voice broke on the final word.

Unable to stand it anymore, Michael stepped closer to her and pulled her tightly to his chest. Without any invitation, his hands rubbed her back in small circles, feeling her rigid muscles under the thin shirt she wore. "Don't worry, Jocelyn. It's just a car. It can be replaced. I'm just glad that you're okay."

"I don't have the money saved yet. Blondie had to stay running until I had the money. But now she's gone, and I can't, I can't—" Jocelyn's words dissolved into wracking sobs.

Her distress tore at Michael's heart more than any woman's had before. Probably because she wasn't trying to lean on him or blame him. But he'd done this to her. If he hadn't been so focused on his grandmother's challenge, then Jocelyn wouldn't be hurting in his arms now. This was all his fault, and he had to make things right.

The emergency vehicles arrived, their sirens and flashing lights adding more distraction to the already confusing situation. After speaking with the police officer dispatched to the scene, signing the paperwork, and seeing the tow trucks remove the devastation from the busy road, Michael finally had a chance to catch his breath. Somehow, he'd managed to lose sight of Jocelyn when the EMT took her to the ambulance to check her out.

"Mr. Cavanaugh, your car is over here," a man spoke directly in front of him.

Michael's eyes raked over the now-empty scene in front of him before coming to rest on the man dressed in a chauffer's uniform. Of course, Genevieve had hired him a driver. She knew Michael would need the extra time to make arrangements for fixing this situation he'd caused. So much destruction, all because of a momentary lapse in his attention. Not acceptable in his book.

"Where's the girl who was with me?" Michael asked the driver.

"I didn't see any girl. You were speaking with the officer when I pulled up, but the other drivers had already picked everyone else up." The man spoke quietly, his eyes remaining focused on Michael in an unchallenging manner as if he were ready to take another direction.

With a slight tilt of his chin, Michael said, "Very good, then. I need to get home. Did Genevieve give you directions?"

"Yes, sir. Right this way, Mr. Cavanaugh. I'll have you home in no time at all." The driver turned on his heel and proceeded to open the back door for Michael.

As they drove, Michael had already decided to ask Genevieve to find out the address of where Jocelyn had been taken. He had to make things up with her. And he knew exactly what he needed to do.

JOCELYN

Having someone drive her around, while pretty unusual, made her extremely uncomfortable. How could she possibly let a veritable stranger take her back to her house? The man continued to look expectantly at her. He looked professional, but she didn't know him.

Never get into a car with a stranger; wasn't that what her parents continually drilled into her head as she grew up? But what about taxis or other car services? Did those count? Surely not. Still, Jocelyn felt reluctant to accept the generosity of strangers. Even handsome strangers; somehow, that made it even easier to decide.

"This way, ma'am," the suit-wearing man said. He gestured for her to enter the car, where he held the door open for her.

"I'm sorry you wasted a trip out here. I'm heading over to the market right here, so I don't need a lift. But thank you anyway." Jocelyn took a step back, stumbling as her heel hit the curb, making her arms pinwheel in the most unseemly and embarrassing fashion.

Luckily, she caught herself before anyone rushed forward to touch her. Parts of her remained unsettled after Mr. Cavanagh had held her in such a familiar way. She would never have dreamed he would have a tender or caring side. Maybe she'd misjudged him.

With a quick glance toward where the officer still spoke with the man foremost on her mind, she decided she needed to make a quick escape. If he chose to come and talk with her, she had no idea what would come out of her mouth. After the way she babbled and cried before, she didn't want to embarrass herself any further.

With a parting wave toward the chauffer, she turned on the ball of her foot and managed to make a semi-graceful departure across the grocery store's parking lot. The sudden movement forced her to realize the accident might have caused some soft-tissue damage after all.

The stiffness in the side of her neck started to radiate down into her shoulder, making her think she should pick up some ibuprofen since she was already getting the cat food. At least the walk would help her to work out the kinks.

Walking as fast as she could without drawing unwanted attention, she sighed with relief when the store's door slid shut behind her. For some reason, just that simple whooshing sound seemed to signal a reprieve to her. From what, she could only guess.

Okay, if she were being honest with herself, she simply wanted some distance between Mr. Cavanaugh and herself. Firmly pushing that thought from her overly active imagination, she grabbed a cart and leaned on it as if her life depended on it. The shopping trip took twice as long as it should have because her mind refused to stay on track; it kept showing her mental pictures of Mr. Cavanaugh with a caring and concerned manner over her well-being.

She even chuckled out loud as she realized he actually *did* know her real name. He'd called her Jocelyn at least twice. So, his blatant use of the unwelcome nickname had been a trick to keep her unbalanced. Now that she was on to him, she wouldn't take the bait anymore.

By the time she had her few groceries packed in the paper bag, darkness had fallen outside. Staring out the glass door in dismay, she watched the sheeting rain come down, leaving rivulets on the glass as it slammed into the building. The weatherman had predicted the arrival of this tropical storm for several days, but couldn't it have held out for another half an hour? She didn't need this right now.

Cursing herself for sending the driver away, she sighed and made the plunge into the storm, instantly getting soaked. With shoulders hunched in an effort to keep the paper bag dry, she paid little attention to her surroundings. If she still had her car, she would be home in just two minutes. The wind, rain, and blowing debris caused her walk to take almost fifteen agonizing minutes.

Her fingers shook with cold and probably a little shock as she tried to press the key into the dinky lock. The door swung open just as the bottom of the soggy paper bag gave up its fight to remain intact. Jocelyn wanted to cry with frustration, but it wouldn't do any good. Besides, it would probably alarm the neighbors into calling the police. She could already imagine how Mrs. Abernathy next door would overreact.

The cold and wet exacerbated the growing stiffness throughout her body. Stifling a groan of pain as she started to bend over, she hastily changed her mind and used her toe to simply scoot the few groceries far enough inside to allow her to close the door. Since nothing needed refrigeration, it could all wait until she took a nice, long, hot shower.

Maybe then she could process the day's disastrous events in some relative comfort.

CHAPTER 4

JOCELYN

A sharp pain in her neck woke her. So much seemed wrong. Shivering began to flow through her limbs, and she wondered why she felt so cold. With sleep still clouding her mind, she cracked one eye open to take in the room around her.

Instead of seeing her simple, sparse bedroom around her, she saw an odd angle of her equally plain living room. Using her elbow to leverage herself to a fully seated position, she realized she had never made it to her shower, let alone her bedroom last night.

The last thing she remembered was sitting down on the edge of her sofa to take off her sodden shoes. Looking down, she noticed both of her shoes still remained on her feet, but one of them at least had a shoelace untied.

An unusual sound came from across the room to her left. Turning her head, gasping at the sudden pain flaring through her skull, she sought to identify the noise. Squinting her eyes in the darkness, she saw something small moving across the floor.

Immediately, her mind went to a rat, but the building manager assured her that they'd been eradicated months before she moved in. Small comfort that brought her when she knew one now resided in her apartment regardless of the manager's promise.

"Meow Meow," she called out, thinking her cat could at least corner the rodent until she could find something to contain the problem on her own. Even blind, the cat could still smell, which made her wonder why the rat would choose her place to make its home. Just as she started to despair about her cat not showing up, she realized the rodent actually was her cat after all.

True to her name, she lifted her face from where she ate something on the floor and gave out a tiny, welcoming meow, quickly followed by a second sound unique to her. Jocelyn always considered that sound the cat's special greeting just for her. Relief flooded through her just as her curiosity got the better of her.

"What are you doing over there?" Jocelyn asked. With a grunt of pain, her abused muscles reluctantly moved when she scooted to the edge of the couch to get a better view. Reaching over, she flipped on the light, squinting in the sudden glare, she wiped away the tears which sprang to her eyes before identifying what the cat had gotten into.

"Oh, Meow Meow! You've made such a mess, but at least you found something to eat on your own." The cat had managed to rip open a large gash in the side of the cat food bag, low enough for the food to waterfall out of its confines.

"What did you do? Were you playing with the kibbles?" Looking around in dismay, she could see just how far and wide the cat had managed to spread the food. With the amount of kibble on the floor, she'd probably still be finding the food for weeks to come. "What a catastrophe," she mumbled, chuckling at her own lame joke.

As her mind began to come back to awareness, realization crashed down over her. Her damp and cold clothes directly resulted from Blondie being totaled in the intersection just hours before. Maybe she should be concerned about falling asleep so soon after the accident. Although, the EMT assured her that she had not sustained a concussion.

That didn't give her much assurance as she realized all of her muscles felt abused, even ones she didn't know existed. All of them protested the slightest demand she put on them as she spotted on the floor the bottle of ibuprofen she'd purchased but never actually got around to taking. That probably accounted for the level of pain she felt right now.

Grunting with effort, she retrieved to bottle of pills from the floor and made her way across the living room and into the galley kitchen. Taking a pill had never been so excruciating yet welcome at the same time. A glance at the microwave clock made her groan with dismay. She only had a couple more hours until she had to get up and go to work.

Just the thought of it made her wonder if she should splurge on calling a taxi or leave early to have enough time to walk into the office. Already strapped for cash, she realized she didn't really have a choice. She'd walk. Besides, the exertion would help unkink her body.

Ever since college, it seemed as though one thing after another kept going wrong in her life, whether directly or indirectly. Knowing her dream of a new car had just got put on hold, she decided to spend her lunch hour looking for a used car in the classifieds. Hopefully, she'd catch a break and find something decent.

Her mind refused to dwell on it any longer. Every fiber of her body wished for a reprieve. She needed to lie down, but first, she had to get out of her damp clothes and get warm. Something she'd intended to do hours earlier.

Taking off her blouse, she noticed something strange on the back as she went to set it down. Pulling it closer, she realized it was a smudged handprint. Immediately, she knew exactly when that had happened.

Her cheeks warmed at the idea of Michael being so familiar with her during her distress. She blushed harder as she realized she had mentally called him by his first name as if they were somehow already friends. One twist of fate and a remarkable show of kindness hardly qualified them as being friends. Besides, she knew his type, and she steered clear of them.

Still, as the warm water washed down her back, she imagined Michael's hands as they moved over that same part of her body. A shiver of excitement raced through her body, so unlike her usually calm and collected self. She didn't normally go after the bad-boy type, so what made her think differently about Michael?

As she toweled off, she paused and looked at her reflection in the mirror. Down across her collarbone and again on her left hip, she cringed at the bright purple bruise spreading across her creamy white skin. The crash's impact must have pulled harder against her body than she realized. With a gentle prod, she rubbed her index finger over the imperfection, thinking it was a wonder that this was the worst damage caused by the accident which totaled Blondie.

Granted, the poor old car probably wasn't even worth the front fender, but it was hers, and it had been paid for. Now she was gone.

With a rueful shake of her head at the senseless loss, she brusquely wiped the tear which escaped her eye. It seemed so stupid to be crying over a silly car. Clearly, she needed to get more sleep. Everything always seemed better with rest.

MICHAEL

Michael dismissed the idea of hiring a private investigator to locate Jocelyn's home address, thinking it seemed creepy in a stalkerish kind of way to show up at her house uninvited. Still, he wished he could at least call her and make sure she was well. He hated how they hadn't had a chance to say goodbye, briefly wondering if Jocelyn had planned it that way.

Never in his life had he had to work so hard to get a woman to take notice of him. Quite the opposite, he usually spent most of his time discouraging their attention. For some inexplicable reason, Jocelyn reacted differently to him than any other women in a way that both puzzled and excited him.

As Michael sat in the parking lot of Jocelyn's job, he toyed nervously with the envelope in his hands. He hoped his kind gesture would be received in the way he intended it and not anything creepy. Yet Jocelyn could go either way with both of his gifts for her. He had to make things right with her after all the damage he'd brought into her life.

His grandma's words kept replaying in his mind. "Find someone who understands real estate." Jocelyn definitely fit the bill. Would she be willing to give him a shot? Did he dare to risk her rejection? Of course, he'd go through with his plan; his grandma's life literally depended on it.

Opening the door to the new car, he leaned against the side of the car, straightening his suit coat in an old nervous gesture he'd thought he'd gotten rid of many years before. Chuckling nervously, he realized his hands shook in anticipation of speaking with Jocelyn in the next minute or two.

This, too, was a new sensation. He was usually over-prepared for everything he went after. He hadn't felt this way since telling his father that he was striking out on his own away from the family business. Pushing that unpleasant conversation away from his mind, he concentrated on what he would say to Jocelyn.

The day's humidity swelled all around him, the rains may have stopped, but it left behind the moisture to make it feel like the air contained more liquid than oxygen. Having delayed long enough, Michael pushed himself away from the vehicle and strode across the parking lot. Each pounding step in discordant harmony with his racing heart.

As soon as he entered the lobby, the crisp coolness inside seemed a balm to his nervousness. As per his usual, his eyes scanned the work crew searching for the familiar slim form and short bobbed hair, which he'd come to appreciate increasingly over the last few months. His first perusal came up empty as he failed to see her. Where could she be? Her punctuality and perfect attendance had always impressed him, yet she didn't appear to be here just when he wanted to see her.

Disappointment raced through him, more than he anticipated. Another thing that startled him was he realized just how happy he had been just thinking about seeing her again. He turned to leave but caught movement out of the corner of his eye. Jocelyn.

Concern ripped through him as he noticed her hunched posture and the flashing of her eyes. What had Mr. Bandy said to her to cause her to get upset? It didn't even make sense since she usually seemed so unflappable. Her flushed cheeks reminded him of how she'd looked just after releasing her from his impromptu hug the night before.

The stilted way in which she walked, lacking her usual grace, disturbed him the most. Maybe the accident had hurt her more than he had realized. Clearing his throat to catch her attention, he plastered a smile on his face, even if he had to force it to stay there through his alarm.

Jocelyn looked up and immediately looked away as if she were searching for a place to hide from him. "Jocelyn," he spoke across the room, drawing the attention of all of the office workers to the scene unfolding in front of them. He knew this type of attention displeased Jocelyn as he now received the look of disgust she'd had when she left her boss's office.

His grandma always used to say in for a penny, in for a pound. He held up the envelope and announced, "I have something for you." Even though her eyes narrowed suspiciously, he could tell his statement had intrigued her, yet her gait did not speed up as she made her way across the large room.

When she came close enough, his eyes raked over her body. The one thing which stood out above all else was the bright purple bruise just peeking out of the high neckline of her blouse. She'd gone to some effort to conceal her injury, but he knew where to look. He had an exact match to it on his shoulder. More than anything, he wished he could kiss away the pain at the same time as guilt washed over him for doing this to her.

"How are you feeling today?" he quietly asked when she stopped across the counter from him.

"Like a truck ran me over. How about yourself?"

Her matter-of-fact tone spoke volumes. Deciding to keep this encounter as professional as possible, he dropped the envelope on the counter and pushed it toward her with his index finger. "With how sore I felt this morning, I thought you might like to use this."

Jocelyn glanced to the side hastily, toward Mr. Bandy's office, before she reached out and slid the envelope the rest of the way to her. She didn't make any effort to open it but simply toyed with the corners of it nervously. "I can't accept gifts from our customers."

"You don't even know what it is. Besides, I'm not here as a customer. I'm here as a concerned citizen."

Jocelyn snorted in the most unladylike manner and shook her head slightly. She ripped open the envelope's flap and drew out the two massage certificates. The flush on her cheeks deepened and sank down across her neck.

Uncomfortable with the silence, Michael said, "I thought a couples' massage would help you out."

Jocelyn dropped the papers as if they had caught on fire, her eyes whipping up to meet his. "You can't be serious! You think I'd want to get a massage with you?" Her voice rose at the end of her sentence.

Michael realized they had the undivided attention of everyone in the room. Still, her assumption startled him into exclaiming his denial. "What? No! Not with me!" He sighed, trying to regain some of his usual composure. In a quieter voice, he reassured her by saying, "I thought you and your boyfriend could use them."

"Oh," Jocelyn replied, looking down at the table, unable to meet his gaze any longer.

The last thing Michael wanted was to embarrass her, but this had all gone so wrong. Deciding to try to smooth things over, he asked, "Could you come outside so we could talk?

There're a few things I need to get cleared up from the accident." Looking pointedly around her, he added, "Besides, I think we've entertained your co-workers quite enough for one morning."

Jocelyn slowly looked over her shoulder, wincing in pain even as she made the gesture. Picking up the papers from the counter, she tapped the edges of them on the Formica surface as she tried to make up her mind.

Michael could practically read her thoughts as they raced across her face. He'd never spent this much time actually watching her; it was a fascinating study. He remained perfectly still, not wanting to pressure her in any way and possibly scare her off. His business taught him to be patient. The first one to talk was the first to lose. Michael didn't like losing.

CHAPTER 5
JOCELYN

"**I**'m taking a short break," she announced to the office at large. Her hands fiddled with the small gift, feeling foolish for accusing Michael of an inappropriate advance. Her mind reeled with the stupidity of it all.

How could she have jumped to that conclusion so hastily? Hadn't her mother always taught her to think before she spoke? She wished she could blame her abhorrent outburst to sheer exhaustion, given that her sleep had been poor at best. But she knew better.

Michael always seemed to rub her the wrong way. She'd made so many conclusions about who he was that this new side of him had her off-kilter. For some reason, she felt compelled to clear the air with him.

As they walked out the front door, an unusual occurrence for her, she squinted in the bright sunshine, using its brightness as an excuse to keep her eyes downcast. "Just so you know, I don't have a boyfriend. And thank you. The massage will help. I thought I wouldn't be able to get out of bed this morning, but the walk to work helped me to loosen things up quite a bit."

"You walked to work? Jocelyn, please tell me you live nearby." Michael stopped dead in his tracks, turned on his heel, and grabbed Jocelyn by both arms in his alarm. With her grimace of pain, he just as swiftly let her go, but he remained rooted to his spot while he waited for his answer.

"It's not far," she replied in a whisper. His touch hadn't actually hurt her, but it did cause her to feel the same spark of recognition as she'd felt right after the accident. She craved his touch and immediately felt its loss when he let her go.

"How far?"

Michael's tone let Jocelyn know he would not let this go. She sighed and looked anywhere but at him as she answered, "It's only about two miles."

"TWO!" Michael shouted, instantly stopping himself and continuing in a calmer tone, "Why didn't you call your driver?"

"I don't have mon...," Jocelyn stopped herself short. Anger erupted through her that she felt the need to explain her pitiful situation to him. Michael had no right to be upset with her. "Look; if I want to walk to work, then it's none of your business." She crossed her arms defensively and lifted her gaze to meet his.

"Well, you won't have to walk anymore," Michael answered, his words clipped with barely restrained anger, or maybe frustration. He lifted his hand and pointed across the parking lot.

Jocelyn's gaze followed his gesture and saw a brand new Tesla with dealer plates still on it. Not comprehending his intent, she asked, "You're planning to drive me to and from work?"

"It'd be better than you risking life and limb to walk here. But, no. That's for you. It's not right that you should have to be inconvenienced in any way because I totaled your car."

"You bought me a new car? A Tesla?" Her eyes raked over the sleek lines of the silver car, her heart raced with a thrill of excitement at the idea of owning something so amazing, but then reality stepped right up and burst her bubble.

Jocelyn laughed out at the absurdity of his attempt to make things right. Was he so out of touch with reality that he believed this was a fair trade? She didn't know how much that car cost, but it had to be thousands of times more expensive than her crappy little Honda Civic.

"What's wrong with a Tesla? It's one of the safest vehicles on the road. Besides, you'll never have to spend another cent on gas. It's a win-win. Come on. Just sit in it and let me know how you like it."

"Mr. Cavanaugh, you can't be serious right now." Although she followed Mr. Cavanaugh across the parking lot, she stopped several feet short of the vehicle. With her feet firmly planted and her arms crossed defiantly, she declared, "There's no way I'm accepting *that* car as a gift. It's way too nice, and I couldn't afford the insurance on it anyway. You'll either have to return it or keep it to replace your car."

"I can't return it, and I've already replaced my car as well. You'll just have to take it."

Jocelyn tore her gaze away from the beautiful car to look over at Michael. Just thinking his first name brought heat to her cheeks, which she would say was from the heat outside if anyone called her on it. What would happen if she did take the car? "I guess I could always sell it." Jocelyn bit her bottom lip to keep from grinning at Michael's sudden frown.

"Why would you sell it? It's perfect for you." Michael reached out, stopping himself before touching her arm.

Jocelyn stared at his hand, wondering what it would feel like to have him touch her again. Would she feel the same thrill of excitement, or had that simply been the after-effects of the accident? Shaking her head, she answered, "I don't have anywhere to charge it at my apartment complex. Besides, I already told you the insurance would be way too expensive."

She choked back saying anything more. The last thing she wanted was to tell him just how broke she was. It wasn't any of his business.

"I'll have a charger installed. Please, Jocelyn. Take the car."

"Now you're just being ridiculous. I'm not going to have you paying for a charging station on top of everything else. That's just stupid. Besides, I'm sure my manager wouldn't agree to it anyway." Uncrossing her arms, she started wildly gesturing as she spoke, her frustration with him needing some sort of outlet.

He seemed sincere in wanting her to have this car, but it just couldn't happen. What would her co-workers say? Heck, what would her parents say? The last thing she wanted to tell them was the truth about the accident. They had enough to worry about as it was without her adding more drama.

"I'll talk with your manager. If he disagrees, then I'll just buy your building. I want to make this right with you. Besides, I can't stand the idea of you walking to work. It's just not safe."

With her eyes widening at his outburst, she finally lost her patience. Rounding on him, she looked him straight in the eyes and raised her voice to say, "Mr. Cavanaugh! Do you hear yourself right now? How I get to work is none of your concern."

She hoped that would put an end to this conversation. She knew he had just gotten started from the steely expression that came over his eyes. Well, she could be just as bull-headed as he was. He just didn't know what he was getting himself into.

Not restraining himself this time, he reached out and gripped both of her upper arms as he declared, "It is now! I'm the reason you don't have a car, and I won't allow you to be without something reliable. And please call me Michael. Mr. Cavanaugh is my father."

His final word caught her off guard, causing her hot reply to gurgle to a halt in her throat. The bitterness in his tone as he spat out the word father almost shattered her. What had happened with his father to make him so bitter?

Still, she needed to do something, say something to end the crazy conversation. Breaking eye contact with him, she looked pointedly down at where his hands touched her. At complete odds with what her heart wanted, the logical part of her brain made her say the words, "Please let me go. I have to get back to work."

"Forget work!" Michael's expression became even more intense.

His hands practically vibrated against her skin, stirring something up inside her, but she tamped it down immediately. Managing to maintain a somewhat reasonable tone, she replied, "Some of us have to work, Michael."

There, she'd said his name out loud, and her heart beat even faster. What slight breeze stirred around them brought the scent of his cologne to her, and she inhaled the musky, masculine scent as if it were oxygen to her parched soul. She needed to get some space from him, or she'd do something stupid like accept the outlandish car.

"Please, Jocelyn. Just borrow the car then. We can work out something different if this one just won't do for you. I need to know you're safe after—" Michael clamped his mouth shut, closing his eyes and mind against something painful.

"Are you okay, Michael?" Jocelyn barely even registered her hand moving up to touch his stubbled cheek. Her body didn't feel like she owned it anymore, not with Michael's passionate plea stirring a deep need to protect him from whatever had hurt him.

The instant she made contact with his skin, Michael's eyes flew open and locked onto hers. His hand came up to cup hers against his face. "Please?"

His plea seemed to come from his heart. How could she possibly say no? "Fine, but only until we can make other arrangements. I don't want this in my name or anything. Are we clear?"

Jocelyn pulled her hand away from him and stepped back from his grip. She needed some space to clear her head. Why had she agreed to anything? What was wrong with her?

A pleased expression transformed Michael's face the instant she agreed. The pain slipped away as if it had never been there. Jocelyn wondered if he had just played on her emotion again. Had she just fallen for another trick of his?

Feeling anger stir up inside her, she gestured with sharp motions as she said, "You know what? Just forget it; forget everything. We can let insurance handle everything, and then we don't have to worry about anything. Sound good?"

Michael didn't even seem phased by her sudden change of mind. Instead, he asked, "Why don't we go out to dinner tonight, and you can tell me what you consider a suitable car?"

"Are you asking me out on a date right now?" Now she knew he was playing with her. Her anger continued to simmer at the idea of him making a fool of her. "I have to go." She tried to step around him, only to have him immediately block her path.

"It's a business dinner, Jocelyn. Nothing more. I promise to be the perfect gentleman." He held up his hands, for all she knew, pretending to appease her.

"Are you not even hearing me, Mr. Cavanaugh? Now, step out of my way so I can return to my job. You know, the way I pay my bills?" She glared up at him, her arms crossed tightly across her chest and her foot tapping angrily on the hot pavement.

It looked like Michael was trying to suppress a grin, only making her angrier. She felt ready to scream out her frustration, but she was not about to give him the satisfaction. Instead, she stared at him unblinkingly until he gave ground.

"At least take the keys so you can drive home tonight." He held out the key fob, his eyes practically pleading with her to agree.

Jocelyn stared at the fob as if it had turned into a snake, ready to bite her at any moment. Shaking her head until her short hair flew out in all directions, she answered, "Nope. No way! If I take that, you'll turn it on me and say I accepted it permanently. I know how you work, Mr. Cavanaugh, and I won't be played."

He dropped his hand without any further petition. "Fine," he agreed, his tone still gentle. "What time should I pick you up from work?"

"What?"

"For dinner."

"Are you not even listening to me? What part of 'I don't want anything to do with this' were you not understanding?"

With a quirk of one eyebrow, Michael replied, "You never said you wouldn't go out to dinner with me. You only said you wouldn't take the car. Now, what time should I pick you up?"

Blowing out a quick breath in frustration, Jocelyn glanced down at her watch. She'd already spent ten minutes arguing with him out in the heat of the morning. If she agreed to his ludicrous offer, then maybe he'd leave, and she could always cancel on him later in the afternoon. "I'm off work at five."

"Maybe you should give me your cell phone number so we can coordinate," Michael offered reasonably.

"You know the number at my work. You've certainly called often enough." Jocelyn stepped around Michael, who didn't try to stop her this time. Without a backward glance, she strode back into the cool interior of her office building. For once, she appreciated the drastic drop in temperature, if only to alleviate the redness in her cheeks, which gave a visible sign of her frustration with Michael.

CHAPTER 6

MICHAEL

Michael suspected Jocelyn would try something to get out of their date. When he returned to her work, he drove around to the back door, thinking this was probably where the employees would exit for the day. As per his usual, he arrived thirty minutes early.

With the window down, he inhaled the lemon scent of the magnolia tree under which he'd parked. It reminded him of Jocelyn's vanilla perfume and caused him to smile in anticipation of seeing her again. Since he had so much time on his hands, he fiddled with the display panel to find out the new features of this Tesla model.

His phone vibrated to let him know it was five minutes to five. Rather than be caught playing with the car's features, he turned off the display and rested his hands against the steering wheel. His fingers drummed impatiently against the edge, only causing him to feel more nervous about whether or not he'd misjudged Jocelyn.

Just when he was about to start the car and pull around to the front of the building, he saw the back door opening slowly. Staring intently across the short distance, he saw Jocelyn's attempt to exit the building furtively. His instinct had been correct.

Exiting the vehicle, Michael leaned against the fender, arms crossed over his chest, watching Jocelyn take several steps away from the door along the edge of the building. "Going somewhere?" he called out.

When Jocelyn jumped in fright, Michael's grin widened, not even bothering to hide the fact that he'd caught her in the act of trying to ditch him. He believed in facing things head-on, putting all his cards on the table, and seeing where negotiations went from there. At least all the cards he was willing to divulge, he mentally amended.

Michael watched Jocelyn's expression change from guilt to irritation. Her hands clenched into fists, but her steps changed direction to come toward him. "What are you doing back here? This is only for employees," she asked when she stopped several feet from him.

"I just thought I'd be helpful and pick you up from the employee entrance. Is that so bad?" Michael's hand caressed the hood of the car, his fingers liking the silky feeling of the clean paint but wishing he could touch Jocelyn's skin instead. This errant thought threw him off his game, distracting him from whatever Jocelyn just said.

"There's something seriously wrong with you, Mr. Cavanaugh," Jocelyn said, her arms folded again over her chest.

He loved her feisty pose; it brought all kinds of ideas to his mind, none of which were appropriate for her work parking lot. "You weren't trying to sneak away, were you?" He accused.

"What?" she instantly asked before her lip trembled slightly on one side. "Maybe." She kept glancing over her shoulder back toward the employee exit.

"Let's get out of here, okay? We can talk like two adults over dinner. I've got a reservation at the French Bistro at five-thirty." Michael pushed himself away from the fender and walked around the front of the car to open the passenger door for her.

"There's only one adult here," she mumbled as she stomped past him and dropped into the seat.

Shutting the door softly, Michael turned away before chuckling at her comment. He couldn't believe she'd gotten into the car without more fuss. Her scent immediately filled the vehicle, muddling his mind further. The way she kept looking at the door gave him the clue he needed.

"Can we hurry?" she asked as soon as he sat. Her gaze never left the back of the building.

"Your wish is my command." He put the car in drive and stepped on the throttle. Racing out of the parking lot in the same manner he always did, he didn't think anything of it until he glanced over to where Jocelyn sat, wide-eyed and clutching her seat belt as if she were about to die. "Are you okay?"

Breathlessly, she said, "Do you always drive like this?"

Michael frowned. Glancing from her back to the road. "Like what?"

"I don't know. Crazy?"

He chuckled, almost ready to dismiss her concern. "This isn't crazy. Do you want to drive instead? I could pull over, and we could switch seats." He looked around for a place to pull over when she answered, her voice still sounding alarmed.

"No, no. Just try to keep some space between the front of our car and the back of theirs. Jeez, this isn't NASCAR, you know," she said, pointing ahead, her eyes glued to the scene in front of them.

Seeing her truly afraid caused him to slow down and increase the distance from the car ahead. He never really thought much about driving other than just getting to where he needed to be. But seeing her actual terror, he felt properly chastised, although her final comment amused him.

"I'm sorry for scaring you," he spoke into the silence. Staying on his best behavior for the rest of the drive seemed to allow her to relax enough to release her death hold on the seat belt. That was a good sign, at least. Pulling into the reserved parking space of the French Bistro, he didn't think anything of the parking attendant opening the doors for them.

"Oh, um, thanks," Jocelyn stammered as she exited the car and met Michael at the front of the vehicle. "Am I dressed okay for this place? I mean, it's pretty high-end. Maybe this wasn't a good idea." She grabbed his arm in her rush of words, lending more intensity to her simple statements than she probably intended.

Michael only then realized how posh this place would seem to her. Having been a regular customer since the doors first opened six years before, Michael didn't even notice the décor anymore. Yet, looking at it from her perspective, he wished he'd thought of someplace else to take her to put her more at ease.

Taking in her pretty blouse and nice slacks, Michael reached over to put his arm around her shoulders. Leaning toward her, he whispered, "You look perfect. Stunning, really. Let's go inside, and you'll see." With only a little prodding, he got her to move alongside him. He liked how small she felt next to him like he could shield her from the world and make everything perfect for her.

This unbidden thought caused him to flinch. Luckily, they'd reached their table, and it was time to let go of her anyway. Still, she looked over at him with her head cocked as if to ask what had just happened.

Michael cleared his throat as a distraction and addressed the hostess, "Thank you. This table is just perfect." He gestured for Jocelyn to sit in the booth across from him before taking a seat himself. Of course, this was the table they reserved just for him, but he didn't have to tell Jocelyn that right now.

"Have you been here before?" Jocelyn asked, picking up the menu and reading it intently, shifting it to the side to catch the light from the candle.

"A time or two," Michael answered nonchalantly.

"Oh, good. What would you recommend?"

"How hungry are you?"

Her shoulder lifted slightly, and her head marginally tipped as she answered, "Not very."

"The steak tartare is nice."

She wrinkled her nose and shook her head. "I prefer my meat cooked."

"Okay, they've got a good Coq au Vin and gratin dauphinoise. They could pair it with a nice white wine if you'd like."

"That sounds fancy. What is it?"

Michael grinned and answered, "Vegetable stuffed chicken and scalloped potatoes."

Jocelyn chuckled as she set her menu down on the table, folding her hands over it as she leaned forward to say, "Jeez, why don't they just say that? Sure it sounds great. What are you having?"

Just as he opened his mouth to answer, the waitress stopped at their table, her eyes raking over Jocelyn before coming to rest hungrily on Michael's face. "Will you be having your usual, Mr. Cavanaugh?"

"Yes. But isn't it customary to take the lady's order first?" Michael reprimanded the woman, not appreciating her rudeness toward his guest or how she looked at him like he was her dessert.

"Yes. I'm sorry." She turned away from Michael, having the grace to blush at her faux pas. "Madam, I could go over today's specials or answer any questions you might have."

With an accusatory glance at Michael, she shifted her gaze to the waitress and ordered what Michael had recommended. As soon as the woman left, Jocelyn rounded on Michael and loudly whispered, "What was that all about?"

"Her? She knows better. I merely—"

Jocelyn rapped her index finger on the table and shook her head before interrupting, "Not that. I thought you said you'd only been here a couple of times. I'd hardly say that qualifies for having a regular meal that the staff already knows." She continued to glare before her eyes widened. Leaning forward even further, she asked in hushed tones, "Do you own this place?"

"What? No!" Michael defended himself, although he couldn't stop himself from laughing. Just her expression alone would have caused him to be amused, but her assumption that he'd own this place simply put him over the edge. He leaned back in his seat and said, "But that isn't a bad idea."

Seeing her incredulous look, Michael took pity on her and answered, "I'm friends with the owner. I come here just about every day when I don't have business take me out of town. I like the food."

He shrugged as if to indicate that was all there was to it. He didn't want to share that he hated eating alone, and he wouldn't cook only for himself.

JOCELYN

Sitting back in her seat, she watched Michael closely. What wasn't he telling her about this place? What else didn't she know about him? Deciding now was as good a time as any, she thought she'd turn this meeting around on him. Besides, knowing what she did about him, he'd probably enjoy talking about his favorite subject.

"So, besides real estate and fancy cars, who is the real Michael Cavanaugh? What do you do in your spare time?" she asked.

His reaction surprised her. Not only did the smile freeze on his face, but he also seemed distinctly uncomfortable. Gone was his easygoing nature, replaced by a facsimile of his usual self.

Picking up his napkin, unfolding it, and placing it precisely on his lap, he avoided eye contact with her. "Free time is a luxury I don't get to enjoy very often," he replied quietly.

"Surely, you don't spend all your time working," she pursued.

"That's true. But I'm with my grandma any moment I don't spend on finding my next land deal." His mouth clamped shut as if he had divulged too much information with that simple sentence.

He almost seemed relieved when the waitress dropped off a basket of bread and a dish of olive oil. Rather than voice anything else personal, he pretended to be inordinately occupied with selecting the perfect slice of bread, although they all looked the same to her.

The smell of fresh-baked bread wafted over to her, making her mouth water and her stomach growl loudly. In an attempt to cover up the sound in the silence surrounding them, she hastily asked, "Do you realize this is the first real conversation we've ever had?"

Reaching over the table, her fingers randomly plucked a bread slice from the basket so she could see if it tasted as good as it smelled. Tearing off a small chunk, she dipped it into the oil and brought it to her mouth, her eyes never leaving Michael's face. The bread practically melted in her mouth. She rapidly tore off another chunk to sample again, whether seasoned with hunger or simply a magical loaf from a supremely skilled baker.

Something about her comment or actions triggered a change in Michael's posture. His inward gaze shifted back to awareness as he stared intently at the motion of her hand. A hungriness in his eyes caused Jocelyn to wonder if she'd erred in directing the conversation to something personal. But she'd started something, and now she wanted to see it through.

"Tell me about your grandma."

He flinched. Absently, his hands tore the bread into tiny bits, which he dropped unheeded onto the small bread plate in front of him. "We're not here to talk about my family."

"Why not?" She asked, plopping another chunk of oil-soaked bread into her mouth, chewing slowly while assessing Michael's strange demeanor. In the short time she'd known him, he'd always seemed so self-assured and poised. This side of him made her wonder what he hid under his over-the-top ego he usually displayed.

"Because we need to discuss your transportation issue. Or more like your lack of it right now." He dropped the bread onto the small plate and folded his hands on the edge of the table, his attention now entirely on her.

"Right. I don't have a car because you said something distracted you while driving. What were you thinking about that you didn't notice you had a red light?" Jocelyn leaned forward intently, bread forgotten for the moment in her hands, her eyes practically begging him to give her a straight answer.

"I just received some bad news about my grandma—" Michael began before clamping his mouth shut.

CHAPTER 7

MICHAEL

Now why on Earth had he brought up his grandma again? Jocelyn's presence must be turning his mind to mush. Yet, even as he appraised her expression, she seemed genuinely interested in hearing his answer. Maybe he could trust her with the truth.

He couldn't risk it. Not yet, anyway. Instead, he decided to hedge the truth just a bit. "I found out my grandma only has six months left to live."

"Michael! I'm so sorry!" Jocelyn's hand reached across the short distance, separating them, and covered his clasped on the table.

Feeling the warmth of her comforting gesture only reinforced his sadness. His grandma had used this same gesture with him ever since he was little. Of course, she wouldn't know about that, but it still unnerved him more than a little bit.

"Can I ask what's wrong with her?" Jocelyn spoke softly into the silence.

"Parkinson's." His voice broke on that single, terrible word, forcing him to cough to regain his composure.

"Oh, that's terrible. My uncle suffered from that for nineteen years. I'm so sorry, Michael. Is there anything I can do to help?"

He knew she meant well, but he couldn't help his sharp reply, "Only if you have a cure. I'm sorry, that wasn't very nice of me. Please forgive me."

Thankfully, their dinners arrived just at that moment. Jocelyn pulled her hand away from him, almost as if she felt burned. She probably did after he spoke so harshly to her when she was only trying to help. Could he work any harder at driving her away from him? He must be flawed inside to be so awful.

JOCELYN

The food provided the perfect distraction for both of them. The aromas alone interrupted the hurt Jocelyn felt when Michael snapped at her. She knew it wasn't personal, but it still stung to be on the receiving end of his frustration with the medical diagnosis.

She understood the pain he felt for his grandma. After all, she worried about her father just as much, even though he wasn't ill. Her father had decades left to live, as far as she knew, not a paltry six months like Michael's grandma.

Once their dinner plates were cleared, Jocelyn decided to break the ice with Michael one more time. After wiping her mouth with the cloth napkin and returning it to her lap, she kept her eyes downcast as she smoothed out the fabric while she asked, "Tell me about your grandma. She must be an amazing woman."

"She is amazing – the best person who ever walked on the planet. Heck, she's more of a mom to me than my own mother." Michael's sudden burst of words came to an abrupt finish. He looked anywhere but over to Jocelyn.

Wanting to keep him talking, Jocelyn shifted gears. "Is she your maternal or paternal grandma?"

"Paternal. Although how she raised someone like my father is beyond me."

"You don't get along with your father?" For some reason, this bit of news bothered Jocelyn more than the grandma's diagnosis. Usually, when grandparents died, the parents would comfort the grandchildren. If Michael didn't have that open, loving kind of relationship with his parents like she did, then she knew he would feel terribly alone during this troubling time in his life.

After pausing for several moments in which Jocelyn started to believe he wouldn't answer, he finally spoke slowly, halting between each phrase as if trying to find the right fit for his words.

"My father is a hard man to like, let alone love. He's—driven by something other than relationships."

"What about your mother then? She saw something in him."

A harsh snorting sound erupted from Michael's lips, entirely at odds with his polished exterior. "Sure. She saw his millions of dollars, his name, and his power. Nothing else concerned her."

"But she had you. Surely, she loves you. All mothers adore their children. Especially those who make a name for themselves, as you did."

Slowly shaking his head, Michael's eyes looked at her with a broken countenance. "She had me as an obligation. My father had a pre-nuptial agreement that she'd give him an heir. Once she had me, she didn't even try to have a spare. When

I was little, I remember hearing her say something about her pregnancy all but ruining her body, and it was the worst thing to ever happen to her.

"No, she never wanted to have children. She was a lousy mother and an even worse wife. Although I hear she's amazing at tennis. She certainly spent enough time at the country club to perfect the sport."

Jocelyn could hardly believe the conditions which Michael described. Her parents would have gladly had a dozen children, but her mother's breast cancer at a young age had ended that dream. Their family spent as much time together as possible, laughing, loving, and enjoying one another's company.

"I'm so sorry, Michael. I had no idea things were so hard for you growing up. Where did your grandma fit into your childhood? Did you spend a lot of time with her?"

"Yes. At first, it was just the summers when I was out of boarding school. But by the time I turned ten, I went to live with her full-time at the family plantation." Michael looked away, pursing his lips as if he regretted sharing so much.

Needing to make him feel more comfortable, she tried to think fast about what to share about herself to make him feel like they had something in common. Unfortunately, she opened her mouth but realized she couldn't think of a single thing.

They indeed came from different worlds. He'd grown up with all the money in the world but a broken family. She'd grown up having to be careful with every dollar they earned, but she had an amazingly strong family. Her mouth snapped shut with an audible click when she dropped her head. With nervous movements, her fingers played with her cloth napkin's edges, and a nick in the side of her nail caught on the fabric.

Suppressing a chuckle, she felt exactly like her fingernail, caught in a snag too big to fix. She had to cut her losses before she got in any deeper with Michael. "I need to get going."

"So soon? Why? We haven't even discussed what we're going to do about your car," Michael spoke rapidly, almost like he wanted to delay her departure.

"I, uh, I've got to get home to feed my cat," she stammered.

"Your cat? Seriously?" Michael shook his head disbelievingly. He tapped a finger against the table's surface as he continued, "That's the best excuse you've got? Do you even have a cat?"

"Yes, thank you very much. Meow Meow has medical issues, and I need to make sure she eats."

"Meow Meow? You can't possibly think I'll believe that. It doesn't even sound like a real name. It sounds like something you just made up on the spot. Besides, what medical issues could your cat have? Diabetes, or something?"

"No, she's blind. And old. She doesn't hear or smell very well anymore, and I really have to make sure she gets enough to eat."

"I give up. If I don't give up now, then Meow Meow will probably end up with so many ailments you won't be able to keep track of them all. Okay, let me get the check, and I'll take you home."

"Oh, you don't have to do that. I—I can walk from here. It's really not that far," she stammered, suddenly realizing Michael would know where she lived if he drove her home. She did not want that. Some of her pride had to remain intact, after all.

"Really? How far is it from here? Oh, let me guess. Only about a mile. Am I close?" Michael's eyes remained fastened across the table to hers, but his arm rose to catch the waitress's attention as she passed by. "Check, please."

Anger flared up inside her as he continued to make fun of her. Maybe he could laugh about her circumstances, but she wasn't finding his scorn a bit funny. "I don't have to take this from you," she whispered harshly, leaning forward even as she scooted sideways to exit the booth. "As I told you before, you can deal with my insurance company about replacing my car. Good evening, Mr. Cavanaugh."

"Jocelyn, wait!" He called out, pausing for a second to throw a wad of bills on the table.

She didn't even try to stop her eyes from rolling at his actions. He probably walked around with more spare money than she had managed to save in the past two years. She knew this had been a bad idea. If he hadn't ambushed her at work, she'd already be sitting in her living room watching re-runs and petting Meow Meow.

People began staring at the spectacle they left in their wake. Surely, her cheeks were blotched with red as her anger continued to simmer without any outlet. At this point, a nice brisk walk back to her apartment sounded like a fantastic idea.

It didn't even matter to her that it was probably over a mile away. Heck, it wouldn't even matter if a hurricane decided to make landfall right now. She probably wouldn't even notice it with her mind already whirling with unkind thoughts toward Michael.

He probably made up that whole sob story about his family life just to make a fool out of her, she decided as she angrily pushed the front door open. Her abrupt appearance startled the man who was supposed to open the door for guests.

"Sorry," she said to him, instantly contrite for her outburst. He wasn't at fault for her foul mood, and he didn't deserve to feel her wrath. Glancing over her shoulder, she realized Michael was catching up with her. He was her problem, but she didn't want to make another scene. Once was enough for one evening.

Lengthening her strides, she swiftly crossed the parking lot and turned onto the sidewalk. The sun stood low on the horizon ahead of her, but the day's muggy heat still made her clothes stick uncomfortably to her skin. She didn't dare turn to see what happened with Michael. With her luck, she'd twist her ankle and have to crawl home in even more misery.

Her ears strained to hear his footsteps. She felt confident he wouldn't just let her walk away, but maybe she was wrong. After all, what did she honestly know about him? Enough, she told herself, her thoughts returning to all of the conversations she'd overheard him having with his business partners — none of them very complimentary to her opinion of him as a person of any excellence.

A car pulled up alongside her, startling her back to awareness of her surroundings. "Jocelyn, get in the car."

"No! Go away!" she replied hotly, only sparing a single glance at Michael leaning across the passenger seat, his wrist over the top of the steering wheel while he continued to roll slowly next to her.

Cars honked behind him as he held up the traffic, some of them angrily pulling around his vehicle. If she didn't do something, she would be the cause of another accident that would haunt her forever. Having come to this conclusion, she noticed a driveway up ahead and pointed, "Fine! Pull over up there. I'll go with you."

She slowed her steps, dreading what would happen when she got into the car. What could she possibly say to him now? How would she handle the embarrassment of letting him know where she lived? The flashy Tesla pulled to a stop across the sidewalk, and Michael got out of the car.

Great, she thought, we're going to have another go out here in public. Just what I need to finish off this fantastic night of horrors. But, to her surprise, Michael merely stepped around the car and opened the passenger door for her. She sank into the seat, waiting for him to make some snarky comment which never came.

His impeccable manners unnerved her. How come she couldn't peg him accurately? She'd never been this bad at reading a person before, and it made her uneasy. This was unfamiliar territory.

He returned to the driver's seat, sitting in silence for several seconds. When he drew in a breath, Jocelyn almost cut him off to give him a piece of her mind. Just as she opened her mouth to let him have it, he said, "I'm sorry, Jocelyn. I shouldn't have made fun of your cat. It was rude and immature. Can we start over?"

Jocelyn let out the breath she'd drawn in for her angry words. His words deflated her anger faster than a dart hitting a balloon. Her parents taught her better than to behave in such a childish manner.

She turned to face him and said, "No, Michael. I'm the one who should apologize. I think we should start over."

"How about we get some gelato? We missed dessert, after all." He raised his eyebrows playfully, for all the world looking like he did forgive her deplorable outburst.

How could she possibly refuse him when he was being so perfect? Hoping she wouldn't regret this later, she sighed and answered, "Okay, but we'll have to make it fast. I do have to get home at a decent hour for Meow Meow's dinner."

CHAPTER 8
MICHAEL

He didn't have any idea how his words would affect Jocelyn. But clearly, he hit a nerve when he teased her. For some reason, he thought they had gotten to the point where he could joke with her, but obviously, he was wrong. Very wrong.

His heart constricted until he clutched at his chest when she abruptly left the table. Seeing the hurt expression on her face told him exactly what went wrong — his mouth. His wisecracks about her cat, which she seemed to love more than he ever thought imaginable, had created the problem.

Of course, growing up, he never had a pet of his own, so he had nothing to compare.

Racing through the restaurant, heedless of the stares of the other patrons, some of whom he knew well, his only thought was how to fix this with Jocelyn. He'd opened up to her faster through dinner than he'd ever done with anyone else before.

She made him feel safe. Something he hadn't felt in a long time. But he had to go and ruin it with his stupid mouth.

Seeing her round the hedge at the parking lot entrance, he knew the wisest course of action would be to follow her in his car. Maybe then he could convince her to stay with him just a little longer. Hopefully. That seemed like a big ask at this point, but he still thought he might salvage something from this perfect evening before he'd mucked it all up.

Feeling impatient at having to wait for a glut of traffic to pass by, he leaned forward, searching the sidewalk to make sure she hadn't managed to take a side street to elude his pursuit. He hoped she would be thinking clearly enough not to do anything drastic, like walk into traffic. If anything happened to her, he didn't know if he could live with himself.

An opening appeared in the traffic; Michael punched his foot on the accelerator, at once missing the roar of a powerful engine. The silence of this electric car almost made him feel cheated somehow. At least with a quiet motor, he could approach Jocelyn without scaring her. That was one good thing to think about.

In anticipation of speaking with her, he fumbled with the controls until he figured out how to roll down the passenger side window. Only half of his attention was on the traffic ahead of him, probably not the wisest choice given how he'd run into Jocelyn's car only the day before because of such a distracted mind.

Still, seeing Jocelyn stomping up the sidewalk with the sun silhouetting her just perfectly made him think she looked like a goddess who was ready to catch the sunbeam back home. Really? He thought to himself. When did he start getting such fanciful ideas?

Finally, he pulled up alongside her, leaning toward her as far as his seatbelt would allow. "Jocelyn, get in the car," he said with authority but trying to sound as reasonable as possible. Fear once again raced through him, thinking that this could quite possibly be his last chance to speak with her again.

Her instant refusal to follow his order didn't give him much hope for a different outcome than his worst-case scenario. In his mind, only she existed in the world right now. So focused had he become on this frustrating woman, he didn't even hear the horns honking or notice the angry gestures from the cars passing him on the left. They didn't matter. Only Jocelyn mattered, and he needed to convince her of that fact.

When she suddenly relented and told him to pull over up ahead, he just barely restrained himself from cheering. His pulse raced in anticipation of making this right. But he had to tread carefully with her.

At least he'd learned something from this evening. She'd been hurt in the past by someone, and she protected herself by running. Much like himself. Maybe they shared more in common than he imagined. He'd certainly like to find out.

He felt anything but calm as he opened the door for her and let himself back into the car. An apology seemed like the right place to start. His grandma would undoubtedly agree. Noticing his fingers shaking, either with excitement or nerves, maybe both, he gripped the steering wheel in an attempt to still his rising panic.

Words spilled from his mouth, but he never even heard what he said. It almost felt as if someone had taken control of his mind for a few seconds, directing him to speak what was on his heart rather than treating this like the business transaction he'd mistakenly told himself this should be. Jocelyn meant more than that to him now. All he had to do now was convince her. Easy. Right?

He blamed the vanilla scent of her perfume on his muddled mind. She had him under some sort of spell. The funny thing was, she didn't even know she was doing it.

Maybe his grandma had been correct in telling him to look for someone who understood his business. Jocelyn definitely fit the bill. She knew more about land records than he did, and that spoke volumes to him.

The car's interior remained silent on their drive to The Gelato Shoppe. His grandma had introduced him to this little dessert shop almost twenty years before. Coincidence? Probably not. Besides, he needed to feel his grandma's wisdom on him right now if he wanted to work through this tough patch with Jocelyn.

Something in his distraction must have shown on his face. His attention immediately came into focus as soon as Jocelyn began speaking.

"What are you thinking about? You look like you're a million miles away." The spoon of chocolate gelato remained suspended in the air as Jocelyn waited for him to answer.

He watched a thick chocolate droplet fall from her spoon to land back in the little paper bowl. "My grandma," he blurted. "She used to bring me here after school when I was a kid."

"Ah. I was wondering how you knew about this place." She looked his body up and down appreciatively before adding, "You don't seem like the type to indulge in sweets."

For some reason, her appraisal of his physique didn't make him feel dirty. On the contrary, it made him thankful he'd kept his personal trainer on retainer after Angelica had left him. Smiling his first genuine smile since dinner, he answered with a chuckle, "Oh, I've got quite the sweet tooth. Just ask my grandma."

"I think I'd like to meet your grandma. She sounds really special," Jocelyn spoke offhandedly just before plopping the oversized bite of gelato into her mouth. "Oh!" she mumbled, waving her hand in front of her face excitedly.

"What's wrong?" Michael asked, concerned enough to rise from his chair.

"Sit, sit. It's just brain freeze," she answered, pressing her palm against her forehead, eyes tightly scrunched shut in agony. "Man, that hurts. That'll teach me to be in such a hurry."

"We don't have to hurry," Michael said.

Managing to open one eye enough to glare at him, Jocelyn only said one word, but she filled it with malice. "Really?"

"Oh, right. The cat," Michael replied, trying not to sound too disappointed.

"Don't start with me again, Michael," she warned.

"At least we're back on a first-name basis. That's progress." Michael took a hasty bite of his vanilla gelato to cover his disappointment. After swallowing, he said, "You know, I've never had a cat before. I'd like to meet this Meow Meow, who has you so loyal."

"Hmph." She tipped her bowl and scraped the last bit of chocolate together onto her spoon. After licking the melted dessert off, she pointed the plastic utensil toward him and said, "I'll tell you what. You can meet Meow Meow if you let me meet your grandma." She quirked one eyebrow as if to challenge him to agree.

He didn't even have to think about his answer before saying, "It's a deal." He stuck out his hand for her to shake on it, a broad smile spreading across his face at her shocked reaction. Wriggling his fingers to speed her up, he felt as if some small bridge had been crossed between them.

When her palm came to rest against his, his fingers automatically curled around her delicate hand. He never imagined the silkiness of her skin could affect him in such a manner. It almost felt like an electric shock of recognition shot through him.

Gazing across the table, he thought he could see the same reaction on her face. Their eyes remained locked on one another, both of them forgetting all about their surroundings as long as their hands remained in physical contact.

The raucous laughter of a group of teenagers entering the store broke the strange spell which kept them enthralled. Jocelyn glanced away like she'd been caught doing something wrong. She withdrew her hand as if his touch burned her.

At once, Michael felt her loss. He wanted to take her hand back, bring it to his lips, and savor her scent. But he didn't do anything except let his hand drop to the table. Clearing his throat, he said, "So, let's go introduce me to Meow Meow. I sure hope I'm not allergic."

Jocelyn instantly burst into a fit of giggles, a merry sound he'd never heard from her before. He couldn't imagine his offhand comment being that funny, but she obviously thought so as her giggles swiftly became hiccups.

"What was so funny?" he asked when she seemed to have recovered sufficiently.

"Nothing really. I think I'm just wound up and tired," she replied, waving away his question.

Michael noticed she didn't make eye contact with him. His comment had meant something to her. Unfortunately, she didn't trust him enough with the truth. Maybe she'd tell him eventually, but he wasn't about to press his luck at the moment.

JOCELYN

The part of the evening she dreaded finally arrived. More than anything, she wished she could just call a car service to come and get her. She didn't want Michael to see the dumpy little apartment complex in which she lived. Good grief, most of the time, she didn't want to admit it to herself either.

Still, her common sense won out over her pride. A ride with Michael would be free, not to mention much safer and more pleasant than riding with a stranger. Just the idea of sitting next to him in the fancy car and drinking in the scent of his sexy cologne almost drove her to distraction.

And with how sore her body still felt, she could not even consider walking home. That little jaunt up the sidewalk had let her know every muscle which felt abused from the accident. If her battered muscles felt this stiff today, she almost groaned in dismay over how she'd feel in the next couple of days.

How could she have come up with that crazy deal? Better yet, why did she shake on it and make it official? Michael must have slipped something in her gelato when she wasn't looking. Ever since he began speaking with her, she'd stopped making rational decisions. This was so unlike her usual self.

What was it about him which caused her to become so scattered? Did he feel the same around her? Glancing up at him from beneath her lashes, she mentally shook her head. No way, he seemed as confident and composed as ever. He didn't seem to have a clue how he affected her. Well, she wasn't about to feed into his ego and let him know.

Grabbing up her purse, she scooted her chair back, flinching as the metal feet screeched along the checkered floor tiles. "Are you ready to go?" Daring to make eye contact with him, she felt her heart jolt with the desire she saw smoldering in his eyes. It only lasted for a split second before he smiled, and a mask of politeness dropped over his expression.

"Sure thing," he replied, standing up without his chair making a sound.

He seemed so eager that Jocelyn wished she didn't have to take him into one of the worst parts of town. Not that this town had much crime, just poverty. And she was a poster child for the impoverished. Maybe she could make one last plea to dissuade him.

"I could just call an Uber or something. I'm sure you have better things to do than drive me around town," she said, shrugging to make it seem like she didn't care either way.

"Nope. No way. I'm dying to meet your cat. Besides, I cleared my evening to spend it with you." He stepped up to her side, bumping her shoulder playfully with his arm.

"Kind of presumptuous, don't you think?" She turned to look up at him. Why was he suddenly so interested in her? This drastic character shift had to be about more than just replacing her car. It seemed more personal.

"I'm ever the optimist. It hasn't failed me yet." Holding the door open for her, he grinned foolishly at her until she passed by him.

Just as she reached the car, Michael scooted around her to open the door for her. "You don't have to do that, you know?"

"Be a gentleman? Of course I do. My grandma would tan my hide if I neglected my proper duties in the presence of a lady."

Taking a seat in the car, she looked up at him with a grin forming on her lips, "I'll be sure to tell her how wonderful you learned your lessons from her." With a quirk of an eyebrow, Michael shut the door and went around the front of the car.

Jocelyn couldn't help but appreciate his profile as he walked around the car. Her eyes seemed drawn to him like he was air to breathe, and she was oxygen-deprived. He carried himself with such confidence, which she used to think of as arrogance.

But, now that she'd had a chance to get to know him a bit, she wondered what type of man he truly was. After all, his grandma played a big part in his upbringing, and she grew up in a long-forgotten era.

CHAPTER 9

MICHAEL

"So, where are we heading?" he asked as he fastened his seatbelt. Feeling more than a little curious as to why she kept coming up with excuses for him not to take her home, he waited anxiously for her answer.

"Head up this street and take a right at the light," she answered, gesturing with her hand unnecessarily.

Seeing her long, slim fingers reminded him of his grandma. She'd always had such nice hands, from all her piano-playing days she insisted. Pain ripped through him at the thought of losing her, causing him to inhale sharply.

"Are you okay?" Jocelyn asked, turning to face him with such an expression of concern.

It made Michael feel foolish for 'borrowing trouble' as his grandma liked to say. Here he was, sitting in his car with a fantastic woman, and yet his mind kept turning toward the macabre. Plastering a smile on his face, he did his best to concentrate on the moment at hand. "I'm fine."

To distract himself, he asked, "Anything I should know about your cat before I meet it?"

"*She* is very friendly once she gets to know you. But don't expect to have her greet you at the door. She's not like a dog. It has to be on her terms before she'll grant you an audience."

Michael didn't miss Jocelyn stressing the pronoun. He'd have to be careful not to refer to her as an 'it' in the future. "Sounds like a diva to me."

Jocelyn snorted before replying, "She's a typical cat. Haven't you been around cats before?"

"Nope."

"Surely your grandparents had barn cats or something."

"Nope. I think my grandpa was allergic to them, or maybe he just didn't like animals. We never had any on the plantation."

"Tell me more about this plantation. Did they work the land? Turn left at the next light." By now, Jocelyn had turned to lean her side against the door so she could see Michael easier.

He liked the idea of her wanting to get to know more about him. It made him think he might actually have a shot at getting a second date with her. If he kept her asking questions, then he might get to know more about her own motivations.

Making the required turn, he realized they were headed to the poor part of town. He already didn't like this. Hopefully, they were only passing through for a shortcut.

"No, my grandparents had a lot of money from good stock purchases. The land has been in the family for many generations, and my grandma liked the idea of letting everything grow wild. She enjoyed sitting on the porch and watching the deer eat the wildflowers that sprang up from the seeds she'd sown every fall."

Jocelyn sighed wistfully and said, "Sounds idyllic. Do they still live there?"

"No. My grandfather died several years ago, and my grandma moved into an assisted living facility several months ago. She's eighty-nine now, but don't you dare tell her I told you that!"

"What's going to happen with the property? Are you living there?"

Michael spared a glance over to her. She seemed genuinely concerned about the property, certainly more interested in it than Angelica had ever been. "No. I don't live there yet, but I hope to sometime soon. There're a few details that I have to take care of before that can happen."

"Oh! Turn left right here!" Jocelyn cried out, leaning forward to point excitedly.

With tires squealing, Michael just managed to make the turn. "A little warning would be nice. How much farther is it to your place?"

"Sorry; I got caught up in your story." She bit her bottom lip and said, "Um, my place is in that apartment complex at the end of this block. You can park on the sidewalk on the right."

Michael managed to restrain himself from groaning out loud. His worst fears had come to pass. Jocelyn lived right in the middle of what the real estate agents referred to as 'Felony Flats.'

"How long have you lived here?" he asked, trying to act casual all the while his mind screamed at him to do something to get her out of here tonight. He couldn't risk going caveman on her, or she might shut him out again. Pulling the car to a stop, he leaned over her side of the car to peer out her window. "Which one's yours?"

She seemed distracted by his proximity, almost as much as he felt by hers. Having her so close made him want to take her into his arms and feel her melt against his chest. He'd felt it the day before, but they'd both been too distraught to appreciate the feeling.

She fumbled with her seatbelt, and then the door handle as if she felt trapped in the car with him. Immediately, Michael mirrored her action so he could get out and open her door for her. Obviously, he'd gotten too close for her comfort. He'd have to take things slower, as much as that frustrated him. Somehow, he thought she'd be worth it in the end.

Even though he hurried, he didn't reach her side of the car before she let herself out. "You should've waited for me," he mumbled.

"I can use a car door just fine," she protested.

"It's not about ability. It's about respect and honor."

Crossing her arms defiantly, she tipped her chin up and asked, "You think I need to honor you? You do realize this is the twenty-first century, right?"

Michael shook his head and clucked his tongue at her. "You've got it all wrong. It's about me showing you respect and honor for the lady you are. You deserve to have a man wait on you hand and foot."

With her eyes widening with the realization of what he meant, her mouth formed a small circle as a small "Oh" escaped her lips. "I'm sorry, then. I guess I've never really thought about it like that. It sounds pretty nice, though. Even if it is an antiquated way of thinking about it."

"What can I say? I'm an old-fashioned kind of guy." With a grand sweeping gesture of his arm, he said, "After you, my lady. Show me to your humble abode." Even as the words left his mouth, he felt truer words were never spoken. With the paint peeling off of the siding on most of the buildings on the street and a few broken panes of glass, this street looked even less than humble. It looked completely abandoned and neglected.

The humid night air hung limply around them. It appeared even the wind didn't want to inhabit this part of town. Weeds pushed through the cracks in the sidewalk, making the path uneven and treacherous in the low light from the few street lamps that still worked.

Hearing sirens in the distance, Michael had to restrain himself from pulling Jocelyn close to his side to keep her safe. A righteous anger began to stir inside him the more he thought about her walking these streets alone. How could she be so careless of her safety? Didn't she realize how bad people could be?

Jocelyn walked just a step ahead of him, her strides exuding confidence which made him feel proud for some reason. At least she carried herself with authority. That alone might dissuade any would-be attackers. She turned up an equally crumbling staircase and opened the front door. His eyes darted from side to side, ensuring their safety, even if Jocelyn seemed oblivious to her surroundings.

Michael noticed no key was needed to gain access to the building. If this were his building, he'd install a keycard system to keep the occupants safe. At least now he understood why Jocelyn hadn't wanted to keep the Tesla. He'd be lucky if it were still parked out front when he left Jocelyn's apartment later.

The cracked plaster on the hallways did nothing to improve Michael's opinion of the building. He could only hope her apartment had been updated sometime during this century.

Just as they rounded a corner, Jocelyn's footsteps faltered. Her hand rose to her mouth, she whipped her head around, eyes wide, and said, "Oh, no!"

Having his attention so focused on the decrepit building and following Jocelyn, he hadn't looked ahead until now. Instantly, he saw the reason for Jocelyn's alarm, but he hoped the problem was with one of her neighbors. The police tape crossing over the doorway up ahead, solidified his resolve to find a better place for Jocelyn to call home.

"Is that your neighbor's place?" he asked, his hand reaching out to comfort her as she remained rooted to her spot. He felt the tremors coursing through her body, her reaction more intense even than that after the car accident. "Josie? Please talk to me?"

His use of the nickname seemed to have the intended reaction. Her eyes came back into focus only to be replaced by another wash of fear.

"No. That's my place," she stated. Instantly she began moving away from Michael. "I hope Meow Meow is safe," she called back over her shoulder.

"You can't go in there. It's a crime scene," he added pointlessly as he watched Jocelyn charge through the yellow tape and begin calling out for her cat. Michael just reached the entrance where the door stood open at an odd angle with the hinge broken, and the door frame a splintered mess when the door opened across the hallway.

"I'm calling the police! You ruffians can't keep coming in here and expect to get away with this!" the old woman spouted as she used a cordless phone to point at him angrily.

"Ma'am, I'm here with Jocelyn. I'm not the bad guy, but can you tell me what happened?" Michael turned, using his most reasonable tone, usually reserved for complicated house procurements in run-down neighborhoods. He glanced over his shoulder to see if he could spot Jocelyn inside, but he had to deal with this woman before he created more problems for everyone because of his presence.

"How come I've never seen you before? How do I know you're not one of them?" She held the door close to her, ready to slam it shut if Michael made any move toward her.

He saw she still hadn't dialed the phone. Holding out his hands to show he had no weapon, he said, "Do I looked dressed like I've come to rob the place?" Looking back over his shoulder, he saw that's probably what had happened since all the furniture was in shambles along with papers, pictures, and clothing strewn everywhere.

The old woman leaned forward, her eyes squinting as she appraised Michael's appearance. "I guess you do look much nicer than those hooligans. Thank goodness Jocelyn wasn't home when this happened."

"Were you the one to call the police?"

"You bet I was. And Mrs. Abernathy next door as well. It took those officers long enough to get here too. The thugs came and went without seeing the whites of their eyes; they did." She spoke emphatically, spittle flying from her mouth, and her jowls bounced loosely. Her bossy attitude seemed so out of sorts with the rollers in her hair along with the polka dot bathrobe and fuzzy, pink slippers that were at least two sizes too small for her feet.

"Did you get a look at them?" he asked, barely restraining the smile as he took in her unkempt appearance.

"You bet. I see everything around here. For all the good it does. They wore ski masks, black coats, and blue jeans," she reported, her ill-fitting dentures clacking on and off her gums as she spoke.

Michael feared he'd have to rescue her teeth from hitting the floor if she didn't mind herself better. "How many people were there?"

"Two who ransacked the place and a third one standing lookout at the corner," she replied, using the phone to point to where they had just come from.

Michael dug his wallet out of his pocket, pulled out his business card and a few twenties, and handed them to the old woman. "If you think of anything else, or if you see those guys again, call me. Okay? I promise to have someone out here immediately to take care of them once and for all."

"Oh, aren't you just a sweetheart? I'm glad Jocelyn has someone so nice to take care of her now. She's alone way too much, you know. It's not right for a girl her age to be single. You have yourself a nice evening, young man." Her head kept bobbing up and down as she tucked his money into her robe's pocket and shut the door.

Only then did Michael have the chance to go after Jocelyn. His eyes raked over the devastation within the apartment and imagined how Jocelyn must feel right now. To be violated in such a manner would be terribly shocking. "Jocelyn? Are you okay?"

"Yes," he heard her mumble from the next room over. At least her place was small enough for her not to get lost. He followed where her voice came from but failed to see her in the room.

"Jocelyn?"

"Come on, Meow Meow. It's okay, girl. I'm here now. You can come out. Michael, catch her! She looks like she's ready to bolt out on your side of the bed."

Michael didn't even think twice as a streak of white fur did exactly as Jocelyn had said. Unfortunately, he wasn't quite fast enough to catch her body, her slick fur ripping past his hands as she raced away. But he was lucky enough to close his fingers around the end of her tail just before she made a clean getaway.

Feeling smug about his feat, he instantly regretted his actions when Meow Meow took exception to his rough handling. Her body twisted around unnaturally fast, her claws raking unerringly down the side of his arm and the back of his hand. But he didn't let go, much to his surprise, even as the pain from the score marks registered to his brain.

"Don't hurt her! She's just scared," Jocelyn cried out, her head popping up above the opposite side of the mattress.

"Hurt her? She's fine, but I'm not coming away from this unscathed."

"Don't be such a baby," Jocelyn scorned as she made it back to her feet and raced over to rescue the cat from his hold. "She's just defending herself in the only way she can."

Having eyes only for her cat, she looked over the beast, inspecting her for any injuries. "Are you okay, sweetie? Were you so scared?" She crooned over the cat just as a mother would dote over her child, who just fell off the swing set.

Seeing their reunion caused Michael's heart to constrict. Other than his grandparents, he'd never had anyone be so concerned about him before. Deciding to give them some time alone, Michael turned and headed into the bathroom.

Wetting a washcloth he found in the drawer, he dabbed at the blood dripping down his arm.

He'd have quite the permanent reminder of this evening since some of the scratches seemed deep enough to leave a long scar. Using the bar of soap, he cleaned the wounds as best he could, but the bleeding continued pretty heavily in a couple of spots.

"Do you have any bandages?" he called out while still rummaging through the bathroom drawers in his own quest. His movements were hampered by keeping pressure on the wound with the washcloth. He heard some rustling in the bedroom as he continued to search.

CHAPTER 10
JOCELYN

Jocelyn appeared in the doorway a few seconds later, the feline absent from her company. Seeing the splashes of blood all over the bathroom, she instantly grew alarmed. "What happened, Michael? Did you cut yourself on something?"

"Your cat happened," he practically growled. His motions became more agitated as he pawed through another drawer, searching for bandages.

Jocelyn pushed past Michael in the small space, her entire torso having to brush up against his back that gave her a slight thrill even though the situation didn't fit with the emotion. Maybe the break-in had made her hypersensitive to everything.

In any event, she put the lid down on the toilet and pointed for Michael to sit where she directed. Once he complied, she held out her hand to assess his injury herself. Once the washcloth came away, blood began pooling again in two of the four parallel gashes down his wrist.

She could not deny her cat caused the damage; the symmetry of the wounds gave it away even if it were hard to fathom her docile cat acting in such an unusual manner. Replacing the towel right away and using her palm to apply pressure, she said, "Put your hand here while I get the bandages out of the cabinet."

Michael complied. His fingers brushed against hers, causing her to inhale sharply at the electricity that seemed to shoot through her hand, up her arm, and straight to her brain. She pulled away as though she'd been burned, clearing her throat to draw attention away from the strange contact.

She took a small step back, turned away from Michael's intense gaze to open the mirror, and rummaged through the cabinet behind it. With the glass obscuring her face from his, she tried to compose herself enough to deal with him once more. She'd have to touch him again to apply the bandages, but her mind kept wondering if she should allow herself to get close to him or stay away and remain safe.

She almost snorted out loud at the idea of being safe, especially considering her apartment was now an official crime scene. Usually, talking helped her in awkward situations. Grabbing up the gauze and tape from one of the shelves, she shut the glass and said, "You're lucky I collect bandages."

At the same time, he asked, "Where's the cat? Wait. What? Why do you collect bandages?"

Jocelyn grinned sheepishly, feeling foolish for bringing up her strange obsession with anything bandage-related. It wasn't as though she needed them much for herself, but whenever she went to the store, she usually ended up perusing the bandage aisle and buying anything new they had in stock. She had at least one of every kind of bandage at her disposal.

"I put Meow Meow in her carrier. She likes it in there; it makes her feel safe." Jocelyn kneeled in front of Michael, avoiding his question to concentrate on the task at hand. She ripped off several lengths of tape and stuck them to the side of the counter before she unrolled some gauze.

"Did you already wash it?" she asked, still looking anywhere but his eyes.

"Yes."

"That's good. Normally, I'd like to put some antibiotic ointment on it first, but I'm afraid it won't do much good until the blood flow slows down. When I say so, pull the cloth off, and I'll begin wrapping. Hopefully, we can work together quick enough to avoid too much more mess." Looking around at all the blood smears, she thought it looked like more than a simple robbery.

The procedure went as well as Jocelyn could have hoped. Michael's bandage looked pretty good for having an amateur apply it, preventing him from bleeding everywhere. Somehow, he'd managed to keep his clothes clean, a skill she'd never learned to master.

"That'll do it," she announced, pulling her hands away from him and standing up all in one motion. She started to put the supplies away when she noticed her hands had begun to shake. "I should probably clean up this mess."

"No. I don't think so. You need to gather up whatever you want to take, and we're going to get out of here. You've had quite enough trauma for today."

She shook her head, not understanding what he was saying. "I'm not going anywhere. Besides, where would I go, Michael? This is my home." Her eyes darted around to take in the enormity of the task ahead of her.

"You can't stay here, Jocelyn. Didn't you see that your front door is completely broken? It wouldn't be safe for you to stay until that's fixed. Come back to my house for tonight."

"What? No, Michael. I can't ask that of you. Especially after…" she pointed down to his injury. It seemed like a lame excuse to refuse, but her mind refused to work correctly.

Michael stood, seemingly towering over her in the confines of the bathroom. His hands lifted to her upper arms, where he lightly rested them on her. "In case you hadn't noticed, you didn't ask. I offered. I'd never be able to sleep if I didn't know you were somewhere safe. So, let's get Meow Meow and head back to my house."

Shaking her head, she stared into his eyes, wondering if he had some ulterior motive. All she saw was his sincerity and concern. Somehow, this confused her even more. He simply refused to behave how she'd made him out to be in her mind. She had no idea who this kind man was or how she should react to him.

"Just say yes, Jocelyn. No pressure. Just a safe place to sleep tonight. Tomorrow, we can figure out something else if you want to leave right away. How's that sound?" His fingers tightened marginally on her arms, trying to reassure her of his statement.

Letting out a resigned sigh, Jocelyn nodded and said, "Sure. I mean, thank you, Michael. You're going above and beyond tonight. I mean—" her eyes moved away from his to take in the mess around them. "This was not the homecoming I expected."

Tears formed on her lashes without any warning, one of them dropping into a wet streak down her cheek. "I'm sorry. I'm not usually this emotional."

"You don't have to apologize. This would upset anyone. C'mon. Let's get out of here." Michael's hand trailed down her arm until his fingers intertwined with hers. He gently pulled her until she turned to follow after him.

Walking into the living room, she finally saw what he meant. Her initial concern for her cat had blinded her to the disaster of her usually neat house. He was right. She couldn't stay here, at least until the door and frame were repaired.

Picking up the blanket from the floor and replacing it on the back of the couch, she slammed her hands down onto the soft back of the furniture, satisfying her need to hit something, but it still left her feeling empty. "What is wrong with people? What made them think they could come in here and take my things? I don't have anything of any value. This was just for nothing!"

"You're right. Those guys are just scum. They were probably looking for things to sell to buy drugs. I'm surprised this hasn't happened to you before now. This part of town isn't really the best—"

Rounding on him, her eyes sparked with anger; she accused, "So this is my fault now? Just because I can't afford to live somewhere nicer, I deserve to have this happen to me?"

"Jocelyn, stop! That's not what I said at all. We can talk about this later. We need to get out of here now. After all, we did enter a crime scene." He picked up the cat carrier and looked at her with a calm, reasonable expression.

"I'm sorry, Michael. That wasn't fair for me to say. You're right. Let me see if I can find some of my clothes in my room. I'll be right back." She practically ran away, wanting to hide from the words she'd spat at him. How could she have attacked him in such a manner? What was wrong with her?

Rummaging through the mess in her room helped her regain some of her composure. Unable to locate her suitcase, she grabbed a pillowcase and started stuffing undergarments, work clothes, and a few pairs of shoes. None of it would match for all she knew, but it kept her hands busy.

Leaving her room, she entered her bathroom, once again feeling alarmed at the amount of blood drying everywhere. Doing her best to work around it, she grabbed her makeup bag, hairbrush, toothbrush, and toothpaste and shoved them into the already full cloth bag.

Taking a deep breath, she turned to leave. Her eyes caught sight of her reflection in the mirror, clearly showing her the stress etched into the tension around her eyes. She turned out the light and left the mess behind her.

"I think I've got everything I need for now," she announced, brandishing the bag out in front of her.

"You know, I'm surprised the police didn't try to contact you. Don't you think that's strange?" Michael asked, his hand reaching out to take the bag from her.

She let it go without any resistance. His comment finally registered in her scattered brain. "You're right! I wonder if they did try to call me. I had my ringer turned off." Her hands patted down her sides, panic rising again as she realized she didn't know what had happened to her phone or purse. "I'll be right back!"

Racing back to her bedroom, she fell to her knees at the far side of the bed. Surely she had her purse when she came inside the apartment. She probably dropped it on the floor somewhere nearby with her attention on locating the cat.

Her hands roughly pushed bedding and clothing out of her way, almost crying out in relief when she spotted her small handbag. Clutching it to her chest as if it were a lifeline, she tilted her head back, eyes closed, and whispered, "Thank you."

"Are you okay?" Michael asked from the doorway.

Feeling foolish at getting caught, she turned toward the door, seeing Michael's body silhouetted. Pushing herself up by using the edge of the bed, she answered, "Yes. I realized I forgot my purse. Actually, I didn't know what had happened to it, but I found it right here." She stupidly pointed down to the floor.

Recalling why she'd needed it, she dropped it onto the bed and opened it up. Pulling out her phone, she tilted it until the seven missed call notifications appeared on the screen. "I guess they did try to reach me. I should call them back," she said, her thumb already poised over the screen to swipe it open.

"Do it from the car," Michael insisted.

"Right. Good idea. Let's get out of here." She hurried across the room and led the way out of the apartment. Now that she had it in her head to leave, she couldn't get out of the place fast enough. She'd worry about all of this later, but now, she needed a place to relax.

Besides, she had to admit she was more than a little curious about where Michael lived. The closer they came to the car, the faster her heart raced. She had agreed to spend the night at his house.

If someone had told her a week ago that she would be doing this, she would have checked them into a mental institution. Yet, here she was, getting into his Tesla while he put her cat and clothes in the back seat. Life really couldn't get any stranger than this.

MICHAEL

Michael could hardly believe how this evening was ending. When she had walked away from the restaurant, he thought he'd messed up everything beyond repair. Now, she was willingly coming to stay at his house. Only for the night, he reminded himself. Only for a fraction of a second did he consider how the hand of fate had stirred things up in his favor.

Fastening his seatbelt, he started the car and breathed a sigh of relief as the dark streets dropped off behind them. The lights from the sidewalks and storefronts lit every corner, forcing the shadows to retreat under their onslaught and lending a sense of security as they entered the better part of town.

In his excitement, he might have exceeded the speed limit to show her his house, but he didn't mind, and Jocelyn didn't say anything. Glancing over at her, she looked distracted. He could only imagine how he'd feel if his whole life got turned upside down in a matter of days.

"Why don't you take tomorrow off so we can take care of all of the police work?" Michael suggested.

"Oh, that's right! I was going to call the police back. I should do that right now," Jocelyn spoke faster than usual. She seemed fragile, like she was about to break from the tension.

"Sounds good," Michael agreed, reaching over to turn down the radio.

As it turned out, the call was very short. Jocelyn's anger had flared up again, evidenced by her jerky movements and the firm set of her lips.

"What did they say?" Michael spared her a short glance as he neared the red traffic light.

"When I gave them my address, they said the officer might call me tomorrow when he got on shift. She said 'might,'

Michael! Like I didn't matter because of where I lived. Can you believe them?"

"I'm sorry, Jocelyn. I truly am." Michael's mind had already turned to figure out a way where Jocelyn would never have to return to that neighborhood again.

If she didn't want to stay living with him, he'd make sure she lived in a part of town where he wouldn't have to worry about her every single moment of the day.

CHAPTER 11
JOCELYN

The car rolled to a stop in front of an ornate gate. With her eyes widening in appreciation, she realized Michael would never have an issue with security given this kind of entrance to his home. Silently, the gate opened far enough for Michael to slowly drive up the curving, tree-lined driveway.

She wondered if he wanted her to gain some appreciation for her new surroundings through his unhurried driving. Looking over at him, she only saw him staring intently out the window. Not only did he appear distracted, but he also seemed worried. "What's wrong?" she asked into the silence.

Shaking his head minutely, he answered, "Nothing's wrong. I just wondered how you were doing with all of this. I mean, none of this could be easy on you. And you didn't ask to be ousted from your apartment tonight. Yet, here you are, embarking on an adventure with a veritable stranger."

"Well, when you put it like that, should I be worried?" A grin managed to spill over onto her lips. He did seem worried about her answer like he cared how she felt about staying with him. After all, he probably had girls spend the night pretty often, so this wouldn't seem like a big deal to him.

Glancing behind her to Meow Meow, she wondered how this move would affect her persnickety feline. Being blind made her cat wary of new territory, not to mention it gave Jocelyn anxiety about her welfare. But she couldn't possibly tell Michael she'd changed her mind. She didn't have anywhere else to go on such short notice.

"You know, I think I might call in sick tomorrow. I definitely have plenty to take care of now that my apartment's in shambles. Besides, it might do that officer some good to see the victim behind the robbery. He should know I'm not some druggie who wouldn't know if I'd even been robbed."

Taking her eyes off the cat, she turned to see how Michael had received her statement. He faced her, an approving look on his face.

"Good idea. Plus, I'll love telling the guy off myself," Michael replied before reaching to open his door.

"Michael, you don't have to come with me. I can go on my own," Jocelyn hurriedly replied. Yet, the idea of him wanting to stay by her side did make her stomach flutter.

Pausing his exit from the car, he said, "I wouldn't miss it for the world. Besides, I'll need to be your chauffer tomorrow since I'm the one responsible for your car getting totaled."

He wiggled his eyebrows playfully before nodding toward the back seat, announcing, "Let's get the two of you settled inside. I think hot chocolate might also be in order. I'm pretty sure I can whip that up without making it inedible."

Michael's suggestion of a hot drink made tears spring to her eyes. Memories flooded her mind of her mother greeting her outside on a cold winter day with hot chocolate. Those were the days when nothing terrible happened, and all was safe in her world. She wanted to feel that same way every day, but life kept throwing curveballs at her and keeping her slightly off-kilter.

"Are you okay?" Michael asked, his face right next to hers as he leaned in her side of the car. His hand touched her shoulder to show his concern.

Jumping in surprise at his sudden appearance, she gasped. Somehow, she'd been so inside her head she managed to miss him opening her door. "Yes, I'm sorry. I'm just a little off tonight."

"That's understandable. Head inside; I'll get your cat and your things for you." He gave her shoulder a little squeeze of encouragement.

She felt the heat of his hand radiating through the fabric of her shirt. Just as quickly, her mind wondered how his hand would feel on her bare flesh. Instantly shutting down that train of thought, she nodded and got out of the car.

Michael hadn't stepped back with the speed from which she exited the vehicle in her confused state. Her body stood directly in front of him. His breath whispered down onto her ear, causing chills to race over her flesh. She wanted them to stay like this forever, but then her mind forced her mouth to say, "Excuse me."

The last thing she wanted was for him to move, but he stepped to the side. Instantly, she felt his absence as if the warmth in the air had fled with him. She wanted to reach out and hold him, comforting herself with his solid frame and fantastic smell. But she stopped herself before she made a foolish decision that would only embarrass them both.

Beating a hasty retreat from the car, she didn't even take any time to appreciate the delicate gardens out front. Only the solid, carved double doors made her hesitate. The ornate brass knocker in the middle of the door had the head of a lion, fierce and beautifully crafted. Her finger reached out to touch the detail for only a second before her other hand pushed the thumb latch to open the door.

It silently swung open to reveal a vast foyer with marble floors, a center table bursting with flowers, and a double set of stairs leading to the second floor. The moonlight streaming through the windows overhead gave the interior space an otherworldly ambiance. This entrance could have easily been the setting for an episode of Gone With the Wind in its elegance.

Stepping inside, Jocelyn's mouth hung open as her gaze roamed from one side of the foyer to the other. Doors stood open on both sides, leading into equally opulent rooms. How was this possible?

When she'd imagined where Michael lived, this style never occurred to her. The house looked more like a fairytale setting rather than a bachelor pad. Who was this man? He certainly had more hiding in him than the egocentric man he portrayed to the public.

Just as she finished making a wide-eyed circle in the middle of the foyer, her gaze came to rest on Michael, where he stood framed in the doorway. He didn't attempt to step inside; he simply stood there watching her.

"I'm sorry. I got caught up in how beautiful this is. I had no idea your place would look like this," Jocelyn gushed, her nerves causing her to babble.

"Wait until you see the guest rooms upstairs." He took two steps inside and used his foot to close the front door.

The gesture, while innocent enough, somehow triggered Jocelyn's heart rate to spike. She was now standing inside Michael Cavanaugh's house. Not only that, she had every intention of spending the night here alone with him.

As if sensing her nerves, Michael held up the cat carrier a little higher and said, "We should introduce Meow Meow to her new living space. I think she'll love the sunroom." He began walking, leaving Jocelyn behind, dropping her bag of clothes next to the stairs as he passed them.

More than a little curious to see further into the house, Jocelyn fell into step behind him, following him down a dim corridor. What would her cat do here? Would she attack Michael again?

Michael turned into a doorway on the left and flipped on a light. Jocelyn's eyes immediately took in the crystal chandelier illuminating the glass-enclosed room with shimmering rainbows of color.

The wicker furniture had all been painted white so it wouldn't detract from the beautiful flowering plants all around them. At least now she knew where the flowers on the foyer table had come from.

Turning around to face her, Michael's smile lit up his eyes. "What do you think? Will she like it?"

Stepping into the room, Jocelyn's grin matched his. "There's only one way to find out." She reached forward, ready to take the cat carrier from him.

"Nope. I think I should do it. After all, we didn't get off to a very auspicious beginning. I want her to know that she's in a safe place."

"Why don't we do it together then? After all, I don't want her to think I've given her away."

"That's fair enough," Michael agreed. He set the carrier down in front of the padded wicker loveseat and motioned for her to sit next to him.

The small space made it impossible for her not to touch him as she sat. Of course, Michael didn't even try to make room for her; she noticed with a faint smile. Maybe he felt the same electricity passing between them as she did when they touched one another.

Feeling more than a little self-conscious as she settled in next to him, she tried to keep her focus on her cat rather than the heat radiating from Michael's hip. The next few moments would help her decide if she should spend the night here or possibly call her parents and see if she could stay with them.

The latter choice didn't appeal to her. She didn't want her parents to worry about her living conditions, not when they had enough to worry about on their own. The fact that her apartment had been robbed might never get mentioned to them if she had her way.

Just like ripping off a bandage, she leaned forward to unzip the carrier to get this over. It seemed Michael had the same notion. Their hands collided as they reached forward, both of them then pulling back as though they'd been burned. "I'm sorry," Jocelyn spoke into the awkward silence.

"No, I'm sorry." He gestured for her to proceed as he leaned forward, elbows resting on his knees, hands flopped down between his legs.

Jocelyn's eyes stayed riveted to his hands. She loved how rugged they appeared, even though she knew what line of work he did. They seemed at odds with his profession, which also intrigued her. Her attention sprang back to the present when Michael cleared his throat.

Feeling her cheeks turn hot as her embarrassment at getting caught staring at him, even if it were only his hands, caused her to jolt into action. Practically springing forward, she jammed her fingertip into the carrier, making the cat jump in surprise as well. Instantly, Jocelyn wished she could just crawl under the settee and hide like her cat.

Could this night get any worse? Scratch that. She didn't want to tempt fate with such an offhanded thought.

With more care, she reached over to the zipper and carefully undid the entire top, folding back the fabric as she did so. "It's okay, Meow Meow. Mommy didn't mean to scare you. Do you want to come out and check out your new temporary home?"

She stroked the cat's head as it popped up from the carrier. The cat turned from side to side, whiskers twitching as if she were deciding whether or not it might be safe to leave. Jocelyn looked over to Michael, a grin spreading on her face as her hopes rose with the cat's curiosity.

"I think she might like to meet you now." Jocelyn held out her hand for his. Once his fingertips touched her palm, she felt another jolt of electricity pass between them. Luckily, she restrained herself from pulling away and simply enjoyed the strange new sensation.

Drawing Michael's hand forward, she crooned, "It's time to meet someone new, Meow Meow. Be nice this time, okay?" It impressed her more than a little bit that Michael's hand didn't register any hesitation or nervousness at getting near the cat. Her eyes rested on the bandage covering his wrist, and she inwardly groaned for the damage her cat had inadvertently caused.

Before either of them got close enough to touch the cat, she decided to leap from the carrier independently. Both of them jumped at the suddenness of her departure, but Jocelyn rose from the tiny couch to catch her if she decided to make a run for it. But it turned out none of that was necessary.

Meow Meow stepped around the carrier and made straight for Michael. She twined herself around his legs, her purr loud enough for the neighbors to hear. When Michael used his other hand to reach down, she stretched her neck around, sniffed him, and licked one of his knuckles before butting her head against his palm.

"I think she either likes me, or she's getting a taste for a bite," Michael announced, his wonder-filled gaze leaving the cat to look over at Jocelyn.

"I've never seen her take to anyone so quickly. Not even me. I think you have a new best friend." The words had barely escaped her mouth before the cat leaped up onto the couch beside him. With more confidence than she'd ever shown before, she stepped both paws up onto his leg and gave a little meow.

Jocelyn laughed and said, "I think she just asked permission to be on your lap. Lean back and see what she does."

Following Jocelyn's instructions, Michael brought his legs closer together and withdrew his hand from hers. He stroked the cat's back and watched the cat step several times around in a circle before curling up in a ball on him.

"Yep. Definitely a friend for life." Jocelyn shook her head in wonder, thinking she might have to reappraise Michael if her cat thought so highly of him. She was usually a good judge of character. At least now, she'd have some time to get to know him better.

CHAPTER 12

MICHAEL

Michael beamed with pleasure that the cat had chosen to take a liking to him. As he stroked her soft fur, he wondered if Jocelyn's skin would feel as nice. His imagination supplied plenty of evidence to support this idea.

After only a few minutes, the cat decided she'd had enough attention and wanted to explore. Jumping down, she began sniffing her surroundings again. With confidence Michael didn't think a blind cat could possess, she wandered through the plants in the room, rubbing her face against the pots and leaves as she passed them.

"It looks like she's settling in nicely. Do you want me to show you to your room? I imagine you're pretty exhausted after such a strange evening." Michael stood, turned slightly, and offered his hand to where she remained seated.

Feeling her dainty fingers curl around his palm made him feel like he needed to protect her. Having her here in his home certainly went a long way toward giving him peace of mind. At least tonight, he would know she was safe from harm.

If he had his way, she would never leave here. His step faltered as the impact of this idea struck him. Glancing sideways, Jocelyn didn't appear to notice his strange behavior.

Walking back the way they originally came, he saw the house as though through her eyes. The decorations were ornate, definitely fancier than any of his bachelor friends attempted. If he'd learned one thing from his mother, it was how to make a house look like a home. Even though he'd spent very little time in his childhood home, he still had fond memories of pride in how it looked to his friends.

He also noticed some details that didn't please him, like the edge of the hall runner having a small tear. He'd have to look into getting a professional weaver to repair it before it got too bad.

Also, he saw a small indented scar on the side of the staircase. Cringing, he recalled how Angelica threw a whiskey glass against the polished wood when he got home late again. Only narrowly missing his head with her throw, that was the last night they saw one another.

Reaching the bottom of the stairs, Michael bent down to pick up Jocelyn's pillowcase of belongings. She certainly hadn't thought to bring much. Maybe she planned on leaving as soon as possible. Michael would have to figure out a way to extend her stay.

As he started up the stairs, he said, "I'd like for you to meet my grandma tomorrow. What do you say?"

A beautiful smile lit up her face, transforming her worry instantly. "I'd like that very much. After hearing your stories about her tonight, I'd be honored to meet the woman who had the making of you."

One eyebrow quirked at her assessment, although he admitted it accurately portrayed their relationship. He deeply regretted that Jocelyn would never meet his grandfather. He'd been such a fun and loving man who got along with everyone.

On the second floor, he led her along the carpeted hallway. Stopping at a closed door, he turned the knob and pushed it open to present the room to Jocelyn. Turning to face her, it pleased him to see her eyes widen in appreciation for the beauty inside. "My room is across the hall if you need anything."

Placing her bag on the floor just inside, he wished he could carry her across the threshold and help her get comfortable. But that would have to wait until another day when she became his wife.

What? Where had that come from?

Needing to clear his head, he said, "I'll leave you alone now. I'm sure you're more than ready to take a shower and get some sleep. You've had a pretty trying day." He thought a cold shower was probably in his immediate future even as he spoke. "Goodnight."

"Goodnight," Jocelyn replied.

She looked as though she wanted to say something to him; her eyes stayed glued to his. Michael imagined taking her into his arms, but he feared he would scare her away. Instead, he turned and opened his own bedroom door.

Twisting his head around with one last grin for Jocelyn, he entered his room but kept the door open a couple of inches. He wanted her to know his door was open for her if she needed him. He couldn't say that to her, but he hoped she would understand the open-door policy.

He hadn't even taken one step into his room before hearing her door shut and the lock click over. So much for her trusting him.

Oh well, he thought. Baby steps.

She's here in the house, and that's more than he ever imagined possible at the start of this day.

JOCELYN

Jocelyn leaned against the solid wooden door, wishing she could have spoken the words that bubbled up inside her. Inexplicably, she wanted to have Michael hold her in his arms and tell her that everything would be perfect in no time at all. She'd believe it if she heard him say it.

Instead, she hid in this fancy room, which could easily be transported into a fashion magazine. Michael concealed so many more layers than she'd ever imagined. He wasn't anything like she'd pegged him.

Even Meow Meow liked him.

Tears dripped down her cheeks. Why? She didn't know. Maybe it was her way to release the day's stresses. Perhaps she simply felt sorry for herself and all of the bad luck that struck her lately.

Taking several shaky, deep breaths, she pushed away from the door and picked up her meager bag of belongings. Michael had mentioned a shower, which sounded pretty spectacular. Surely, this meant a bathroom would be through the door on the left wall.

Sure enough, the bathroom held even more luxuries than the bedroom. Unfortunately, only a couple of minutes into the shower, she couldn't control her yawning. Giving up, she turned off the water and dried herself with the plush towel. Wrapping it around her body, she didn't even bother trying to find her nightclothes as she walked across the bedroom and climbed up onto the king-sized four-poster bed.

Her gaze traveled across the room to check the door lock. Nothing had changed. Pulling the towel off, she tucked herself up in the satin sheets, flipping her wet hair up over the top of the pillow to keep it from chilling her as she slept. She didn't even remember falling asleep.

MICHAEL

Michael raced through his morning bathing routine, anxious to be out and about before his guest. He hadn't been this excited about waking up early since his last vacation. He pulled his bedroom door open, his eyes automatically checking the door across the hall, expecting it to be closed tight.

His pulse raced with intense fear as he saw the door was already open. Had Jocelyn decided in the night to leave? Had she been too scared to stay in his house?

Two steps brought him to her doorway, only to discover it empty. At least the bed looked slept in, but the door to the bathroom stood open as well. Turning, he raced along the hall and took the stairs three at a time, not even bothering to try to be quiet. He had to make sure Jocelyn was okay. Checking the rooms as he passed them, the emptiness began to press down on his soul.

Panic had taken a good hold of him before he arrived at the sunroom. Fully expecting it to be empty, like all the other rooms, he had to stare for several seconds before he believed what his eyes tried to tell him was true. Not only was Jocelyn still there, but she had also curled up on the couch with her cat and was reading one of the many books from his vast library.

He didn't expect her to explore independently, nor did he think she would be content just sitting quietly. His experience with other women in his life told him that they needed constant entertainment to be content. Yet, here Jocelyn sat, looking gorgeous with the sunlight streaming down on her from the many windows.

"Hey, you," Jocelyn cheerfully greeted him. "Did you sleep well? You look kind of frazzled."

"I thought you'd left. I saw your door open." He blurted out the first thing that sprang to his mind before clamping his lips shut. So much for seeming calm and collected, Michael, he chided himself.

"I'm sorry to worry you," she replied, uncurling her legs and swinging them around until she sat up. The cat leaped off her lap and sauntered toward Michael.

He watched her progress toward him, mesmerized by her slow, swinging steps and her lazily swirling tail. Surely, she just wanted to sniff at him before returning to Jocelyn's lap. Nope. She proceeded to unerringly walk over and rub against his legs before stretching up onto her hind legs, meowing to be picked up.

"Is this normal?" Michael asked, leaning over to oblige the request before her claws dug any deeper into his knee.

By now, Jocelyn sat on the edge of the couch, a frown furrowing her brow. "Not at all. Are you wearing catnip or something?" A corner of her mouth lifted as this thought must have amused her.

Michael shook his head in denial, his arm curled under the cat's body while his other hand stroked from her head to tail in long swipes. "I must look like Cee Lo Green right now," he commented, grinning at how silly he must look.

"Who?"

"He's a singer who has this cat—oh, never mind. Now that I've found you, we should get some breakfast. You must have been terribly bored. How long have you been up?" Once again, Michael had to forcibly stop himself from talking. For some reason, he couldn't seem to keep his cool around this stunning woman.

"Bored? Who could possibly be bored with this setting?" She gestured wildly with her arms, her eyes alight with honest delight.

Her answer struck something inside him. Every girlfriend he'd had needed constant entertainment. None of them were ever content with peace and quiet. They needed activities and vacations to keep them from complaining of boredom.

Who was this woman sitting in front of him? Could she be for real, or was she simply baiting him? Her serene expression and deep, soulful eyes were anything but deceptive.

"You're serious, aren't you?" Michael kept his eyes on hers as he kneeled to set the cat back onto the floor.

"Yes. Why wouldn't I be? You've got an amazing library and a beautiful home. There's so much scope for the imagination here; I could be lost in dreamland for days on end."

The enraptured look on her face told him she spoke her truth. Michael laughed and said offhandedly, "I think you've watched Anne of Green Gables a few too many times. Next thing, you'll be telling me about your window friend upstairs."

Jocelyn stood from the couch, leaving a book on the cushion, and crossed the room. Her eyes lit up with delight, and she said, "I love Anne of Green Gables. I can't believe you knew that quote. No guy has ever known what I was talking about with that one."

"How many guys have you said it to?" Michael asked, suddenly wary as if she had men waiting in the wings for her.

"So many," she replied quickly. "All of them while I was in high school. My girlfriends and I used to binge-watch the series on the weekends." Jocelyn actually broke out into a case of giggles. "You should see your face!" She playfully slapped his bicep and asked, "Did you mention something about breakfast? I'm starving."

CHAPTER 13

JOCELYN

Jocelyn offered to help make breakfast, but Michael adamantly refused her assistance. Instead, she seated herself at the island and enjoyed the show he put on. For someone who said he couldn't boil water, he sure was putting together quite the spread.

For the first order of business, he heated water and mixed it with something in a cup. He wouldn't let her see what he was up to, so she had to guess. When he turned around, a grin lit up his face, and he placed a cup of hot cocoa in front of her.

"I promised you hot chocolate last night, but we got distracted. I wanted you to know that I always deliver on my promises. It's my grandma's secret recipe, so I hope you like it." Gesturing for her to take a sip, he raised his eyebrows expectantly.

How could she possibly resist such an offer? Besides, hot cocoa was her very favorite beverage. Wrapping her cold hands around the mug, she brought it up to her mouth, breathing in the chocolaty aroma before blowing across the surface to cool it enough to drink.

"It smells amazing, but I'm afraid it's still too hot to try." She leaned sideways, trying to see around him to the ingredients he'd pulled out. "What else are you planning for breakfast? I really don't mind helping, you know."

"I may have exaggerated my proficiency in the kitchen." He looked down sheepishly before glancing up to see how she reacted to his admission.

"For the better or worse?"

This time Michael broke out laughing and asked, "Is there something worse than being unable to boil water?"

Jocelyn put the cup down so fast that some liquid spilled over the edge. Beginning to scoot off of the chair, she said, "That's it; I'm helping."

"No, no! I was just teasing. Hey, I want you to know that I took Home Ec in high school. Mrs. Martin made sure to drill it into our thick skulls on how to function well enough not to starve once we made it to college. I'm proud to say I got an A in that class, too."

Looking askance at Michael, Jocelyn asked, "How much did you have to pay her to get that A?"

"Ouch! That hurts. Wait until you try my French toast, then you can tell me whether or not I earned my grade." Michael turned around and loudly clanked around as he mixed ingredients and pulled out cooking utensils. In short order, Michael grabbed two plates and piled them high with scrambled eggs, French toast, and corned beef and hash.

"Feast your eyes on that!" he triumphantly announced as he set one plate in front of her and the other next to her. Rounding the island, Michael seated himself beside her and nudged her with his elbow. "What do you think? Looks pretty good, huh?"

"Well, it's not burned," Jocelyn admitted. The various aromas of the food wafted up, making her mouth water in anticipation. She hadn't eaten breakfast like this since she lived on the farm with her parents. Picking up her fork, she took a bite and closed her eyes in bliss.

Once again, Michael showed her another side to himself that she would never have anticipated. A thought struck her, and she asked, "How much of this was learned in Home Ec and how much from your grandma?"

Michael chuckled again, his mouth already full of a bite of French toast. Once he swallowed, he answered, "You caught me there. This was the usual breakfast I had growing up on the plantation. Grandma made sure I knew exactly how to make it. She said breakfast was the most important meal of the day to get it started right."

"Your grandma is very wise and an amazing teacher. What else did you learn to make?" Jocelyn dug into her food with an unanticipated relish.

"No way am I spilling all my secrets so fast. Besides, I still have to sample your cooking. Fair is fair."

It struck Jocelyn that their conversation sounded like an old couple reminiscing. Sometime in the last two days, she'd lost her desire to hate Michael because of who she thought he was. Now she simply wanted to get to know him better.

"When do you want to leave?" Michael asked.

Deep in thought, his questions seemed to come out of the left field. Immediately feeling foolish for thinking they were something they clearly weren't, she dropped her fork with a loud clang and answered, "Oh, I'm sorry. You must have so much work to do, and I'm holding you up. I can get my things together right now."

Michael's hand reaching over and covering her forearm caused her to halt her abrupt movement to leave. "Slow down, Josie. I only wanted to know when you'd be ready to head down to the police station. There's no hurry. Please finish your breakfast."

With her cheeks blazing hot from embarrassment, she managed to pick up her fork and make a decent effort at finishing. Why did she keep jumping to the wrong conclusions with Michael? Was her thinking so flawed that she couldn't see what was right in front of her?

"A penny for your thoughts?" Michael asked, setting his fork down on his empty plate and reaching to grab his coffee mug.

"That's it? A penny is all my thoughts are worth?" she asked, her sense of humor winning out once again. She took a sip of the hot chocolate and hummed her approval. "This cocoa is amazing." She gestured down to the nearly empty plate and said, "And the rest of the meal as well. You've got a real talent for breakfast."

Michael actually blushed at the compliment. Instead of answering, he picked up his empty plate and took it across the kitchen to the farm-style sink, where he rinsed it off. His posture looked stiff as if she had said something upsetting to him.

"What's wrong, Michael? Was it something I said?" Abandoning the remnants of her breakfast, Jocelyn rushed around the island, wanting to make eye contact with him. Placing her hand on the small of his back, she could feel the cords of muscle bunched up under his t-shirt.

"I thought we could stop off at the police station and then head over to the care facility so you could meet my grandma. How does that sound?" he asked, avoiding eye contact with her.

"It sounds like you're avoiding my question." She waited another second before she could tell he didn't want to discuss whatever had bothered him. "Yes, that sounds perfect. I'll head upstairs and get ready."

Jocelyn turned and picked up her plate, taking the last bite before setting the dirty dish down inside the sink. Her fingers brushed against Michael's, and once again, the spark of electricity rushed through her. Pulling her hand back as if she'd been scalded, she whirled around and ran from the kitchen.

On the second-floor landing, Jocelyn stopped dead in her tracks. Just ahead of her, Meow Meow sat in Michael's bedroom doorway. "Are you exploring, baby?" she asked, stepping forward with the idea of taking the cat into her room.

Just as she reached down to get her, the cat twisted around and hopped into Michael's room. Not to be deterred, Jocelyn followed, her eyes intent on retrieving her cat. As luck would have it, Meow Meow scurried under the far side of the bed.

Not wanting to offend Michael by the cat's decision to hide out in his bedroom, she hoped to extricate the cat before he even knew they had trespassed. Throwing herself onto her belly on the floor, she wriggled her way under the bed as far as she could reach. Wouldn't you know it, the cat had positioned herself just out of reach.

Feeling frustrated beyond belief, she almost cried out to the cat to come to her when she heard Michael's footsteps enter the room. With widened eyes, she shifted her gaze from the cat to where Michael now stood on the opposite side of the bed.

How could she explain herself? Maybe he would simply leave the room again, and she could make her escape unnoticed. Something struck her in the middle of the back, nothing painful but startling nonetheless. She reached back and pulled the cloth toward her face to discover the t-shirt Michael had been wearing downstairs.

Oh, no! What if he decided to take a shower? Her current position landed her squarely in his path. She had to do something fast. When she heard a zipper being undone, that decided her following action.

"Meow Meow, come out now!" she cried, unnecessarily loud. Sitting up, she acted surprised to see Michael, but the shocked look on his face was too funny to ignore. She started to giggle until her gaze wandered down from his face to his bare chest, to his hands holding the tops of his pants, where they froze in the process of pulling them off.

Immediately, she looked away, her cheeks blazing red as she realized how impossible this situation had become. How would she ever be able to speak with him again after getting caught in his bedroom? Her hand rose to shield her eyes, and she said, "I tried to stop my cat from coming in here, but she's hiding under the bed and won't come out.

"I'm so sorry, Michael. I'll leave right now." She used the edge of the bed to leverage herself up but kept her gaze downcast and her other hand covering her sight of him.

"It's okay, Josie. Oh, hi there, Meow Meow. Have you been causing your mama a bit of trouble?"

Michael's comment startled her into lowering her hand to see if the cat had come out from under the bed. Not only had she left her hideout, but she had found her way into Michael's arms. Something about seeing a bare-chested man cuddling her oversized cat caught at her heartstrings.

Needing to escape this whole situation, Jocelyn hurried around the bed. "What am I going to do with her? She can't be invading your space like this. I'm sorry. We'll get out of here now and let you finish…" she looked away from his six-pack and perfect pecks, feeling another wave of heat rushing up her neck to redden her face, "whatever you were doing."

Twirling around, she rushed across the room with the cat clutched to her chest. Fumbling with the doorknob, she finally managed to escape the room and shut the door behind her. "Bad kitty!" she quietly chided before crossing the hallway to her bedroom.

Closing herself in her room, her mind reeled with what she had just seen. Sure, Michael always looked incredible in his designer suits, but to see him half-naked and so remarkably buff—she couldn't unsee that sight. Her heart raced with a thrill of excitement.

Thinking about going to see Michael's grandma made her slightly nervous. She seemed like such an elegant lady who she wanted to impress somehow. Deciding she should probably dress a little nicer than she originally planned, she went over and dumped out the bag of clothes she had pulled up from her ransacked bedroom floor.

With a sigh of disappointment, she realized now she probably should have spent a few more minutes making sure she had matching outfits. Instead, she had to make do with an ensemble that was less than her best but better than the sweats she had been wearing.

Going into the bathroom, she fixed her hair and makeup as best as possible with the meager supplies she had thought to shove into the bag. Biting her bottom lip, she appraised her reflection, thinking it could be better, but it had been worse in previous interviews. This was as good as she could get it considering her circumstances.

Going back to her room, she noticed the cat had made herself at home in the middle of the enormous bed. Hoping she would behave while they were gone, she opened her door and stood in the hall, undecided what she should do next. She should probably leave the door open so the cat could leave the room to find a place to go to the bathroom or eat.

Immediately, she drew in a breath as she realized they hadn't given the cat anything to eat or drink since they had arrived. To make matters worse, she hadn't even given her any medication. Rushing back into the bedroom, she rifled around until she found the package holding the cat's medication. Rattling the bottle, she discovered it was almost empty. Should she ask Michael to drive her to the store to get a refill or wait until she had a car of her own again? Hopefully, it would be soon.

A tap on her open door startled her to attention. "Are you almost ready?" Michael asked, leaning his sexy body against the side of the door, arms crossed to show off his bulging biceps through the tight fabric of his long-sleeved t-shirt.

"Yes. I, uh, just," she stammered, holding out the medication bottle and giving it a slight rattle. "We forgot to feed Meow Meow, and I'm getting low on her medicine."

"Oh, she and I had quite the session in the kitchen last night while I tried to figure out what she'd like to eat."

"Really? Oh, thank goodness. What did you feed her?" Jocelyn moved across the room, her fears somewhat allayed.

"Cooked chicken breast chunks, salad, and green beans. She turned up her nose to everything else."

"Well, no wonder she likes you so much. You're cheating by winning her heart by feeding her. But thank you so much. I must have been quite out of sorts to forget something so major."

"That's understandable given what happened. Come on. Let's get going. It looks like Meow Meow is pretty content for now. We can stop by the store or wherever to get the meds on our way back from the police station." He held out his hand for her to take.

Staring at it, she didn't know if she could trust herself to make physical contact with him again. Yet, if she ignored his friendly offer, what message would that send him? Enough time had passed to make both of them uncomfortable before she nodded to herself and took his hand.

The spark of recognition struck her soul yet again, but she kept her grip firm to embrace the sensation.

CHAPTER 14

MICHAEL

When Michael began to get nervous about Jocelyn meeting his grandma, all he had to do was think about the look on her face when she unexpectedly popped up from beside his bed. He had to restrain himself from chuckling, but the silly grin kept reappearing unbidden. Still, this meeting could be good or bad, all depending on how his grandma felt. On the bad days, his grandma struggled to remember her own name.

His mind drifted back to their encounter at the police station. Just when he thought he'd have to step in and make some threats of his own to the arrogant police officer, Jocelyn surprised him with a backbone of her own. The officer had done a double-take at the docile-looking girl who sat across from him, his brow furrowing in consideration of what Jocelyn had pointed out to him.

He loved a woman who could stand up for herself. He honestly didn't know if Jocelyn had been up to the task, given how nervous she'd been in the car before they entered the precinct. But, when push came to shove, she did exactly what she said she'd do and made sure the officer knew that decent people could live in poor neighborhoods.

He pulled into the reserved parking space and turned the car off. Turning to Jocelyn, his expression suddenly serious, he said, "This is where my grandma is living right now. As I told you before, she's been sick, and they're working on a treatment for her here. I won't know how she's doing until we get in there. Some days are pretty bad. I just wanted to warn you beforehand."

"I understand. What's her name? What should I call her?" Jocelyn unfastened her seatbelt, and Michael noticed her fingers shook slightly, whether from nerves or excitement, he wasn't sure.

"Her name's Evelyn Cavanaugh. You can call her Evie or grandma; she won't mind either." Michael chuckled and added, "Just don't call her Mrs. Cavanaugh. She hates that. She says it sounds too formal for a setting like this."

"Are you sure? I mean, I've never met her before. I don't want her to think I'm being impertinent."

"There you go with another Green Gables reference. C'mon. You'll see what I mean when we get inside." He opened his door and rushed around the car to get hers as well.

It pleased him to see she waited for his assistance to get out of the car. At least they'd made progress on that front. He wanted her to feel like a queen, just as his grandma had taught him to treat a lady of substance. He rested his hand on the small of her back and steered her into the building and out of the day's growing heat.

This time, when they crossed the lobby, he saw the female staff do a double-take that he wasn't alone. Some of the women even scowled with jealousy, which inordinately pleased Michael. That would teach them to look at him like their next meal, or worse yet, their next paycheck.

He turned them down the long hallway, his mind racing through how he'd handle his grandma should she be having a bad day. His feet knew the path they needed to take; he didn't even need to see where he was going. So often had he traversed this path he no longer noticed the surroundings.

Jocelyn suddenly stopped. Her intake of breath brought Michael back to his present awareness. "What's wrong?" he asked, seeing the surprised look on Jocelyn's face.

Her hand rose to point at a particular seascape painting. Michael gazed at the art, thinking the painter had quite the eye for catching the movement of the water as it curled and broke against the rocks.

"That's my mother's painting!" Jocelyn announced. She stepped closer to inspect the details. Raising her finger to the corner, she tapped the frame before looking back over her shoulder to add, "See! That's my mother's signature!"

"She's very talented. Why didn't you tell me about this?" Michael stepped beside Jocelyn, replacing his hand on her back, liking the physical contact. He glanced to the side and noticed this was a commissioned painting. An idea formed in his mind, but he kept it to himself for the moment.

"I didn't know she'd sold anything. She always said it was just for herself. Wow. How cool is that?" Her face lit up with a grin of pleasure over her mother's accomplishment.

"I'd like to meet your mother if only to compliment her amazing talent," Michael said conversationally.

Jocelyn abruptly turned away, clearing her throat nervously. "Um, where's your grandma's room? We should be going. We don't want to keep her waiting."

Wondering what had triggered her sudden mood change, Michael tried to lighten the atmosphere by saying, "She doesn't even know we're coming, so I hardly think she'll mind if we delay for a couple more minutes. Do you think your mom has any other works displayed here?"

"I didn't even know about that one," Jocelyn spoke brusquely, waving her hand back toward the one painting. Still, she avoided eye contact as she spent an inordinate amount of time inspecting the other paintings on display.

Coming around to stand in her way, Michael held onto both of her arms and asked, "Did I say something to offend you?"

A sudden shaking of her head hardly gave Michael any reassurance since she still refused to look up at him. Using an index finger, he placed it under her chin to lift her face until she had no choice but to acknowledge him. "What's wrong?"

She let out a long sigh. "Michael, I promise it's nothing."

"Clearly not true," he stated.

"Fine. I got scared when you said you wanted to meet my mom."

His mind reeled with her answer. It just didn't make sense. "Why?"

"Look, I haven't taken a guy home to my parents' house since my high school prom. It's complicated. Can we just drop this?" Her eyes practically pled her case for her.

Michael knew when to drop something. He'd get his answers later. Right now, she needed something to take her mind off whatever caused her such distress. "Sure. Grandma's room is right over here." He kept one hand in contact with her, feeling as though she were as flighty as a scared deer during hunting season.

He brought her to the door and after a quick rap of his knuckles to announce their presence, he cracked open the door far enough to stick his head inside to check if she were awake or asleep. Seeing his grandma sitting next to the electric fireplace with her knitting on her lap, he smiled and said, "I brought someone for you to meet, Grandma. Are you up for a visitor?"

"Mikey! Of course. Come in. Come in." She set her knitting on the ornate table beside her and folded her trembling hands in her lap, a grin spreading across her face in anticipation.

Michael pushed the door open the rest of the way before pulling Jocelyn from the hallway and into his grandma's view. Just as he'd suspected, his grandma's eyes sparkled with mischief. Today must be a good day for her since she looked like she was cooking up some scheme in her head.

"Oh, who's your lady friend, Michael? Where are your manners? Introductions are in order."

Drawing Jocelyn closer to his grandma, he tipped his head toward Jocelyn and said, "This is my beautiful, amazing, and astute grandmother, Evelyn Cavanaugh. Grandma, this is my friend, Jocelyn Ostinkemp."

Jocelyn stepped forward, hand outstretched as she leaned down to embrace Evelyn's tiny hand. "It's so nice to meet you, Evelyn."

"Oh, please call me Evie. Do your friends call you Josie? I grew up with a girl named Jocelyn, and we all called her Josie. Smartest girl I've ever met. Come, sit down and tell me all about yourself." She never let go of Jocelyn's hand but instead steered her toward the vacant seat next to her. Glancing over to Michael, she said, "That didn't take you long. Good boy."

Michael had the grace to blush at his grandma's not-so-subtle remark. Maybe he should end this before it got too far. He opened his mouth to speak when his grandma beat him to it.

"Mikey, please be a dear and go get us some refreshments. The kitchen has the best tea and cookies at this time of day." Her shooing hand dismissed him as much as her gaze returning to Jocelyn.

Without any other choice, Michael hurried before things got truly out of hand. Maybe he could salvage some of this meeting if he could keep her occupied with serving tea rather than talking.

JOCELYN

Seeing Evelyn sitting like a queen in her private quarters made Jocelyn want to smile. She only had faint memories of her own grandmothers. All of her grandparents died before she turned ten since her parents had waited a long time before having her.

As soon as the door closed, leaving her alone with the kind old woman, Evelyn began grilling her in an intense manner quite different than her previous way with Michael. Jocelyn seated herself, still holding the woman's hand, surprised at the tightness of her grasp.

"How do you know my Mikey, dear?" Her eyebrows raised and lowered as if pulled by marionette strings as she spoke.

Quite mesmerized by her facial quirk, Jocelyn took a second before answering. "Oh, um, I work at the title company Michael uses for his business transactions."

"Good boy. He took my advice after all. The best matches are made with those who understand one another. Tell me, how long have you worked there?" Using her other hand, she patted the top of Jocelyn's hand playfully.

More than a little confused by Evie's comment, she did her best to pay attention and answer the question. "I've been there for almost two years. What advice did you give Michael? And what does where I work have to do with it?"

"It doesn't matter, Josie, dear. The important thing is that you've agreed to be Mikey's wife. I can't tell you how happy that makes me. It gives me a reason to live again. Just thinking about little feet pattering up and down the hallways of the plantation just makes my heart sing. The two of you will have the most beautiful babies."

Jocelyn felt the muscles in her face freeze into place at Evie's words. Evie transformed from a melancholy old woman to someone twenty years younger with a bright future from the moment she entered the room. How could she possibly correct her that Michael was just a friend?

She couldn't possibly be cruel enough to dash a grandma's hopes for her grandson before first talking with Michael. If Evie's condition were as bad as Michael believed, then maybe

Evie wouldn't even remember that she'd been here. That was the one thing to which she could cling.

Still, she couldn't stop her heart from racing at the crazy notion of marrying Michael, even if she had no desire to marry him of all people. Not that Michael even entertained an interest in her in such a way. After all, the only reason he'd been speaking with her was because he'd crashed into her car. There was nothing, absolutely nothing, happening between Michael and herself.

"Oh, Mikey; you're such a dear. Just set that tray down right here and serve us up some tea." Evie never took her eyes off Jocelyn as she continued her previous train of thought, "Isn't he such a dear? You two will be so happy together."

The sound of China loudly clinking together sounded as Michael fumbled with the teapot. He had the grace to look as embarrassed as she felt. Holding out a cup and saucer to his grandmother first, he said, "Grandma, you've got the wrong idea."

"Oh, Mikey. I can see with my own eyes. Have you taken her out to the plantation yet?" She turned, her eyes alight with renewed vigor, and said, "It's just the most magical place. I can't wait to hear what you think of it."

"No, I haven't been out there, Evie," Jocelyn answered, deciding to go along with the charade for a bit longer.

Michael cleared his throat and said, "I'd planned to take her out there after our visit with you, Grandma."

"That's just perfect, dear. Be sure to show her the swing set out back. It's just perfect for little children. Remember the time when you got swinging so high, you got scared? Ernest had to rush out there and catch you before you fell.

"You would've loved my Ernest. Such a good man and husband. He taught Michael all about being a kind and caring man." Evelyn patted Jocelyn's hand one last time before taking a sip of her tea.

"I think we've spent enough time going down memory lane. Besides, I think it's almost time for your physical therapy session," Michael said. He rubbed his palms against his jeans, looking for all the world like he was embarrassed.

The door had only just closed when Michael turned to Jocelyn and said, "I'm so sorry for my grandma putting you on the spot like that."

"Not at all. But she was so excited about it that I'm afraid she'll be disappointed when she learns the truth. I mean, there's absolutely no chemistry between us." Jocelyn clamped her mouth shut, wondering why she'd added that last bit.

She walked away, not wanting to make things even more uncomfortable between them. She kept her gaze trained on the artwork adorning the walls. It still amazed her that her mother's painting was on display.

That's what she'd think about right now. Indeed not the delicious man following her.

CHAPTER 15

MICHAEL

Michael's feet remained rooted to the floor as Jocelyn's words cut deep. Did she honestly feel nothing around him? Maybe his grandma's ultimatum had clouded his judgment where women were concerned.

Although he could've sworn Jocelyn had started to warm to his charms. But her words said otherwise. He guessed he'd have to step up his game if he wanted to win her over.

He pulled out his cell phone and sent a quick text before hurrying to catch up with Jocelyn. His grandma inadvertently gave him a great idea, plus he'd enjoy watching Jocelyn's reaction to his surprise. His plan replaced the spring in his step and gave him a reason to smile again.

Jocelyn seemed quiet in the car, almost as if she wanted to say something to him. He didn't press her but kept his attention on the road. He turned into a private lot several minutes later and parked the car. Only then did Jocelyn seem to come around to pay attention to their surroundings.

"Why are we at the airport?" she asked, her brows furrowed in confusion as she turned to face him.

"Grandma wanted me to show you the plantation property. She raised me to be obedient, so I arranged for us to get an aerial tour of the property. Besides, it's the best way to get a feel for the size of the place. It's too big to go tramping on foot." He looked down at her fancy shoes, a grin spreading across his lips, and said, "And you're not exactly dressed for hiking."

Jocelyn giggled while nodding. "I guess I'm not. Are we really going flying?"

"Yes. I hope you're okay with that. It's actually a helicopter ride." A sudden fear struck him, and he asked, "You're not afraid to fly, are you?"

Immediately shaking her head, a broad smile crossing her lips, she answered, "I've always wanted to learn to fly. Ever since I was a little girl, I'd hoped to get a great paying job out of college so I'd have enough money to get lessons."

Not bothering to wait for Michael to come around to open her door, she grabbed the door latch and said, "What are we waiting for? Let's go."

Michael chuckled at her enthusiasm, shaking his head at her sudden change in mood. This plan was working out even better than he'd hoped. Who knew she wanted to learn to fly? What a stroke of luck!

Once airborne, Michael took out his cell phone to take pictures to remember this special moment. Jocelyn looked adorable with her perma-grin and the large headset over her ears as she kept her face pressed to the side window. Every once in a while, he could hear her sigh with delight at various sights below them.

Michael hated to interrupt her obvious pleasure about twenty minutes into the flight, but he needed to get her attention. Tapping her shoulder, he said into his mic, "We're coming up on the plantation, just over here."

He pointed out his window. In Jocelyn's exuberance to see everything, she flung herself across his lap, pressing him back into his seat. This excursion was working out better than he ever could have imagined.

Pretending to have as much interest in the view, he leaned forward over her, putting one hand over her shoulders. The smell of her vanilla perfume filled the helicopter, but now it permeated his clothing and assailed his nostrils. She smelled like heaven.

"What part is yours?" she asked, turning her exuberant face toward his.

Her luscious lips were only an inch from his own. It took every ounce of self-control not to kiss her right then and there. Tearing his eyes away from hers, he managed to free his other hand from where she'd pinned it against his lap and pointed.

He explained, "The river is the southern border. Follow that all the way around until you can see that large barn. As soon as we cross the river, it's all ours as far as the eye can see." Saying the word 'ours' gave him a ping of pain, wishing it truly could be his with her at his side.

"Oh, it's just beautiful. It looks like a wildlife preserve with all of the lakes, trees, and fields. Just perfect. I can see why you like it so much out here."

He kept himself from flinching at her offhanded remark about the wildlife preserve. His grandma must have mentioned something about it while he'd been out of the room. Curiosity burned through him about what else might have been said when he wasn't around.

Michael reveled in the feeling of Jocelyn's body pressed against his as she remained there for several more minutes. Finally, she noticed something they passed and shot back to her window to keep looking at it. "I think I saw some animals running down there. Do you have any livestock out there?"

"Not out this far. You probably saw some white-tailed deer. There's probably hundreds of them, if not thousands since there's no hunting on the property."

"I'm glad. They look so graceful running free. How many acres is this?"

"Just over thirty thousand."

She turned to face Michael, eyes wide and her mouth rounding into the shape of an 'O' at his remark. "No wonder you said we wouldn't be able to walk it all." Jocelyn turned back to take in the sights, and a chuckle sounded through the mic.

Michael could see the house nearing swiftly, and he hoped Jocelyn would like it as much as he did. Of course, it was rather large and stately, as an excellent Southern plantation house should be, but he thought it was perfect for the setting. He swelled with pride as the white columns and wrap-around porch came into view as the pilot turned slightly to land in the front yard.

They began their descent, the rotors shifting slightly and the sound of the engines changing as the pilot pulled back the power. Within minutes, they had touched down without a hint of a bump onto the carefully manicured lawn. The engine cut off, and the rotors continued to spin with their built-up momentum.

Removing his headset, Michael clapped the pilot on the shoulder and said, "Perfect flight, Carlos. We'll be a while, so make yourself at home. Miss Tessa should have some refreshments if you want to wander back to the kitchen."

Carlos turned around, his teeth even whiter against his dark-tanned skin as he smiled broadly. "Thanks, Mr. Cavanaugh. Don't mind if I do. Miss Tessa's cookies are not to be missed."

"I guess I know where to find you when we're ready to depart. Have a great afternoon." Michael unlatched the side door and let himself down onto the ground. He turned and held out his hand to help Jocelyn.

Feeling her tiny hand in his did something to him inside, something he had never experienced before with such an innocent touch. Yet, she professed she felt nothing for him, which confused him even more. Smiling to hide his troubled thoughts, he asked, "What do you think?"

"This is definitely going to go down as one of my best days ever!" she gushed while holding his gaze with her eyes shining brightly. Turning away, she drew in a long breath, finally letting it come out with a question. "Is this house really where you grew up?"

"Yes. Wait until I show you around inside. I bet I can guess which room will be your favorite." He squeezed her hand playfully.

"Hmm. I might just surprise you. You could have an amazingly organized closet or pantry. Those things are important, you know."

"We'll see. C'mon." He pulled her close until he could tuck her hand into the crook of his arm. Now that he had his hands on her, he would find any excuse to keep that contact going. She practically buzzed with excitement which charged him even more.

Showing Jocelyn around the house turned out to be everything Michael hoped. She had clapped with glee when he showed her the library. Immediately she crossed the Persian rug to the large window seat, turning as she went to admire all four walls lined with shelves full of books. "How long has your family been collecting these?"

"Some of them were brought over with the family when they immigrated to the states. But my family has always appreciated the printed word, so each generation has added to the collection. I don't think I've read even one wall's worth, but I keep trying." Michael laughed at Jocelyn's unbridled joy.

They ended the tour by passing through the kitchen, where Michael grabbed a woven basket from the countertop. Anticipating their next activity, he held open the back door for her and said, "We'll head across the yard to that large oak tree over there."

"Are we going to have a picnic?"

"Yep. You didn't think I'd let Carlos monopolize Miss Tessa's culinary skills, do you?" They walked together, letting the sounds of the birds and insects fill up the silence. Michael remembered letting these sounds of nature soothe his soul on the days when his father would come to visit and leave with some scathing remark.

Setting the basket down beside the tree trunk, he opened one side and pulled out a red and blue checkered blanket. He unfurled it and motioned for Jocelyn to make herself comfortable.

Once she settled to her chosen spot, Michael picked the space right next to her, letting his knee touch her thigh as he pulled the basket close. One by one, he pulled out the various dishes of potato salad, tea sandwiches, homemade chips, macaroni, cheese, crackers, and a bowl of mixed fruit.

Finally, he brought out a glass pitcher of lemonade, the outside already showing signs of condensation against the day's heat.

"Does Miss Tessa always make this much food on the spur of the moment? After trying all of this, I won't be able to eat for a week."

Nodding, he answered, "She does this every day in hopes I'll come for a visit."

"That seems like a waste if you don't show up."

"Not at all. We've got many staff members who live here. Let's just say they all eat very well." Holding up a tiny square of sandwich, dwarfed by the size of his hand, he waited for her to grab one herself before saying, "Bon appétit."

JOCELYN

As exciting as the day had been, Jocelyn still felt anxiety gnawing inside her. Even as she sat next to Michael under the tree, she imagined her life with him. Evie's words had touched her, even if Michael felt nothing for her.

Swallowing her bite, she cleared her throat. How could she bring up his grandma's strange conversation? Should she just drop it? Or would it be better to air the misunderstanding and resolve it together?

Evie's confusion and dementia must have been the reason for Michael's distraction on the day he ran into her car. After all, he had mentioned at the scene that he'd just come from visiting the care facility. It must be devastating for Michael to watch her mental health decline in such a manner.

"What is rolling through that brain of yours? I can practically see your wheels turning," Michael spoke into the silence.

With a guilty conscience, she glanced up between her lashes at him with her chin still down. Now or never, she told herself sternly. Trying to bolster her confidence by playing it off as a joke, she said, "Your grandma's convinced we're getting married. I mean, how silly is that, right?" Forcing a chuckle and an ironic grin, she watched Michael's face transform into a mask of guilt.

"Yeah, about that...," Michael stammered to a halt, letting out a long sigh.

Seeing Michael's distress, Jocelyn reached over to place her hand on his knee. His eyes sprang over to lock onto hers for a split second. She could have sworn she saw a glimmer of hope sparkle in his eyes before he looked away again.

Her heart broke for his pain. She would say just about anything to take his hurt away. Her mother always said she was a 'fixer.' Although Michael had seemed the least likely to need fixing until she got to know him a little better. He put on a fancy suit of bravado and disguised his pain behind his over-the-top ego, but she saw through it all now.

"It's okay, Michael. I understand what's going on, and I'll support you however I can. This is a hard time for you. I get that." She felt pretty pleased with herself for helping Michael through this tough time. That is until he spoke.

"Really? Then you'll marry me?" Michael turned, his hands reaching out to take hold of both of hers. His eyes shined with renewed hope, and a radiant smile lit up his whole being.

CHAPTER 16

MICHAEL

The notion of his plan to bring her to the plantation to dazzle her had worked. His mind reeled with the shock of it all. Beyond all of his previously dashed expectations, she still wanted to help him. Sitting before him was the most amazing woman he'd ever had the pleasure of meeting, and she wanted to be with him. How could he ever get so lucky?

"Whoa! Slow your roll there, mister. Who said anything about marriage?" She dropped his hands like he'd hurt her, but it didn't stop there. As fast as she could, she moved away from him as if he'd suddenly developed an infectious disease.

He watched her walk away, her movements stiff and awkward as her high heels sunk into the soft grass. She didn't seem to notice or care. But Michael's heart felt two sizes too small as the pain of her rejection washed through him.

No longer did he hear the sweet sounds of the wildlife around him. Nor did he even register the muggy heat weighing down his whole body. None of it mattered now that he knew Jocelyn hadn't been lying when she said she felt nothing for him.

He'd been right from the start. This shouldn't be about love. It was safer to keep it as a simple business transaction. Feeling foolish to believe it could be anything other than that, he formulated another plan while waiting for Jocelyn to return.

After all, she needed to come back if she wanted to go home. He understood the art of timing. He'd practiced it enough times during business dealings. This situation was no different.

JOCELYN

In her agitated state, she'd wandered farther than she'd planned. The initial shock of his proposal wore off, but her disbelief that she could be with him amazed her. This perfect setting could indeed be hers to share with him. All she had to do was say yes to a veritable stranger.

What was wrong with her? She couldn't even entertain this crazy plan. If she were to go along with this, she would be as nutty as his grandma. For Pete's sake, she didn't even know Michael, not in the ways that counted, that is.

By the time she felt calm enough to return, she had discovered herself surrounded by trees. With the thick carpeting of leaves, she didn't even see her footprints to get her back. Turning in a circle, everything looked the same around her.

With a groan of despair, she realized she was hopelessly lost, yet she refused to call out like some damsel in distress. That type of action would only play into Michael's oversized ego. He'd surely find some way to call himself her knight in shining armor, which he obviously wasn't.

No, she'd think her way out of this dilemma. When she was little, she'd had survival training at summer camp. All she had to do was delve through almost twenty years of new information to retrieve the old and possibly antiquated lessons.

Looking up to the sun, she noted its location in the skyline. Of course, this would help more if she could recall the house's location on the property as a whole. Stomping her foot in frustration, the heel of her shoe struck the only rock in sight, neatly snapping it in half.

She stared dumbly at the piece of her shoe lying on the trail. Throwing her head back, she let out a roar of laughter at the ridiculousness of the situation. Not only was she lost, but now she had to hobble on a broken shoe. What else could go wrong?

Only then did she realize the stillness surrounding her. No birds chirped, no insects buzzed, just the ominous silence reigned. With eyes wide, she circled once again, this time searching for anything which might endanger her. Reasoning that it could have been her laughter that had startled the wildlife and not knowing what else to do, she put one foot in front of the other.

Hearing sounds of water, she shifted direction slightly to investigate. Maybe she could be lucky enough to find the river at the property's border. Then she could simply follow it until she encountered—what? She actually didn't know if the river would give her any clue at all, but it was something to go on. The only thing she had goings, as far as she was concerned.

With the shadows growing longer and the birds settling in for the night, Jocelyn began to wonder about the wisdom of not calling out for help as soon as she realized she was lost. Then it hit her. Rule number one for survival school: if you're lost, stay put.

"Well, I messed that completely up," she murmured out loud, comforted by the sound of her voice. Stopping for a few seconds, she wished she could find an open field to try to get her bearings. The trees all looked alike and probably kept her going in circles.

Darkness fell with an abruptness that seemed unnatural. With the last bit of light, she could have sworn she saw an opening in the trees ahead. Rushing to get out into the open again, she paid little attention to her footing.

The trunks of the trees seemed to grow unnaturally large. She should have known what this meant, but her mind reeled with confusion. Practically running now, she took four leaping steps before she realized the ground no longer held solid under her weight.

Her foot sank into the ground past her ankle just before her other foot joined it in the miry soil. Fear lanced through her. If this were quicksand, nobody would ever find any trace of her.

She'd be one of the statistics she'd been warned about. Her mother would search for her in every crowd for the rest of her life, hoping beyond hope to find her lost daughter. Or worse, she could be stuck here like bait for a lurking alligator.

"Think, Jocelyn. Think!" she said aloud.

Rule number two practically took up a neon sign in her head: Don't panic. She took a deep, quavering breath and tried to arrest her full-blown terror.

First, she needed to get unstuck. Her shoes were already a lost cause, so she didn't care when the muck claimed them as she pulled first one foot up and stepped backward as far as she could stretch. It might have been wishful thinking, but the ground seemed firmer just behind her.

So occupied had she become with her predicament, she didn't even hear the noise coming from overhead. Her only concern was in freeing herself from the treacherous ground. Three steps later, both of her feet were once again on solid ground.

Relief washed through her at the close call. Leaning against a tree, she felt her legs grow weak, and she sank to the leafy ground, heedless of how dirty her outfit would get. What did it matter? She was already a mess.

If only Michael hadn't brought her out here, she thought bitterly. Then she wouldn't be facing this awful situation. Drawing her knees up, she crossed her arms over them and put her head down to have a good cry.

When the wash of emotion seeped out of her, she realized she was more to blame for her problem. Nobody forced her to run away like some spoiled child. She had been all too eager to go flying in the helicopter. Nope, this was definitely all her fault.

She decided that she'd find a way back as soon as daylight returned, no matter what. Then she'd sit down and listen to Michael. She'd been quick to judge him harshly before, which was unfair to him. When she saw him again, she'd make things right. She had to cling to that hope as the dark silence surrounded her.

MICHAEL

At first, Michael didn't mind Jocelyn taking her time in coming back to speak with him. He used the time to work out the details of his marriage proposal to her. Pulling out his phone, he contacted his attorney and asked him to draft a formal contract.

Once he finished, he heard a buzzing sound nearby. Looking around, he discovered Jocelyn had left her small purse on the blanket where her phone had an incoming call. More than a little curious, he opened her bag and took out the phone.

The caller ID read 'Mom.' He debated answering the call but then decided against it. His first contact with Jocelyn's mom should probably be at Jocelyn's discretion.

Seeing the call go to voicemail, he set the phone back inside the handbag. Worry began to fray the edges of his determination to give Jocelyn space to work out her anger. Knowing her phone was with him made him realize she didn't have any form of communication with her.

What if something had happened to her? As unlikely as it sounded, she could have managed to get lost. After all, she had never been here before and didn't know the lay of the land other than what she remembered during the helicopter ride.

"That's it!" he exclaimed, jumping up and running back to the house. Crashing through the side door, startling the kitchen occupants, Michael's eyes fell on just the person he needed. "Carlos! Get the helicopter ready to fly!"

Ready to comply, Carlos hesitated, then asked, "Is everything okay? Where's Miss Jocelyn?"

"That's the thing. I don't know where she is. I think she might have gotten lost. We need to start an aerial search before we lose the daylight," Michael answered in a rush. He pulled on Carlos' arm to get him moving faster.

Breaking into a run, they crossed the lawn and climbed into the chopper. Every second seemed agonizingly long to Michael as the rotors began to turn slowly. Was the engine usually this sluggish? Carlos pulled up the collective with the minimum power to safely fly to get them airborne.

"Which area should we start with?" Carlos asked into the mic.

"She wandered off to the south, but that was over an hour ago," Michael answered, feeling stupid for waiting so long. The look Carlos leveled him did nothing to dissuade his guilt over the delay.

Carlos clicked several buttons on the control panel. The glass display showed a grainy image of the ground beneath them. Michael's puzzled expression must have been enough for Carlos to announce, "It's the FLIR system we had installed last year."

"What's that?"

"It's a heat-seeking device. As it gets darker, we'll still be able to find her heat signature."

"Carlos, you're amazing!" Michael stopped looking out the window to keep his eyes glued to the remarkable display.

They just had to find her!

Several blips appeared on the screen, giving him renewed hope, only to discover they were a pair of deer racing away from the noisy helicopter.

Night completely fell, but they continued to canvas the countryside. Michael wondered if they had somehow managed to miss her since their circle of searching had gone out much farther than he thought she'd walk with her inappropriate shoes.

Just when he was about to tell Carlos to head back to the house, he saw a red and orange form appear on the screen. It was definitely human. It must be Jocelyn. "Put it down, Carlos! That's got to be her!"

"On it, boss," Carlos replied, all formality gone with the strain of the search. The only area clear enough to land in turned out to be farther from her location than either of them would have liked, but it was the best they could do.

Michael kept his bearings from the FLIR screen as he opened the door the moment the skids touched the ground. He would search around every tree on the property if it meant bringing Jocelyn home. Even if she didn't want to be with him, he had to make sure she was safe. That had always been his goal with her.

"Wait, Michael!" Carlos called just before the door slammed shut.

Growling with frustration at the delay, Michael turned and opened the door, ready to spout off some scathing remark. But Carlos was thinking more clearly than he was at the moment. The blessed man held out a flashlight for him.

"Thanks!" Michael said as he grabbed the light and flicked the switch. The broad beam of light would help tremendously.

"Watch out for the marshes, Michael. They're not too far from where we spotted her. It wouldn't do for you to need rescuing as well."

"Thanks, man. I'll watch my step. Keep the helicopter running, just to be safe. I don't know what shape she'll be in when I bring her back." Michael took off running, the light swinging wildly in front of him as he dashed recklessly through the meadow's tall grass.

CHAPTER 17
MICHAEL

Michael ran unerringly to Jocelyn's location as if drawn by a magnet. When his light shone over her curled up form against the tree, he felt his heart leap for joy but also dread that she might be badly injured. Even though he did not attempt to keep his footfalls quiet, she wasn't moving, and that scared him more than anything.

Crossing the short distance between them, he kneeled next to her, touching her shoulder to get her attention. When she flung her arms out in fear, striking the flashlight right out of his hand where it fell to the bed of leaves several feet away, Michael could have cried out with elation.

"It's okay, Jocelyn. It's just me, Michael. We found you. Are you okay?" Searching for injuries, his hands felt down both of her arms and then down her legs from her knees to her alarmingly bare feet. "What happened to your shoes?"

The panic in her eyes left as she answered, "The swamp ate them. How did you find me?"

"Helicopter," Michael answered abruptly. "Jocelyn, are you hurt?" he asked again.

"No. I'm fine. Can we go home now?"

The flashlight on the forest floor illuminated the setting enough for Michael to see the dirt streaks down her face as if she'd been crying. She must have been scared out of her mind. Grabbing up the flashlight, he didn't bother to ask Jocelyn's permission as he leaned over and scooped her up into his arms.

Only a tiny squeal of alarm sounded from her before her arms circled his neck. Her body relaxed next to his chest with her head tucked under his chin. She weighed nothing, but his heart felt heavy with relief that he had found her alive.

Once again, he realized how different Jocelyn was from other women. They would have protested against being carried, spouting nonsense about weighing too much. Or they would have been crying uncontrollably from the terror of it all. Not Jocelyn. She simply let him help her without any fuss or protest at all.

This scenario had never played into his list of activities for the day, but he would get her home in no time at all. He hadn't thought this would be how he'd get his arms around her. It seemed like the only time she allowed him to touch her was when she was in danger. He'd have to rectify that situation.

He didn't even remember the walk back to the helicopter. His hand opened the door to get into the rear cabin as if on autopilot, where he set Jocelyn down on the seat inside. Hauling himself into the chopper, he shut the door behind him and settled down next to her.

She hadn't made any effort to get secure for the flight, so he reached across her to fasten her seat harness. Then he grabbed the headset from the hook on the pillar and put it over her ears, adjusting the mic so she could speak if she felt like it. Likewise, he got himself situated and spoke into his mic, "Let's get home, Carlos."

"Yes, Sir!" Carlos answered brightly.

The engine's sound changed as Carlos applied more power, and then they were airborne again. This time, Jocelyn didn't try to look out of the windows. Her eyes remained downcast as she stared at her hands clasped tightly in her lap.

Michael reached over and put his hand over the top of her cold fingers. The drastic temperature difference alarmed him, given that it was probably still about eighty-five degrees outside despite the darkness. She had to be suffering from shock, which meant she was still in danger.

Carlos landed closer to the house than usual to allow Michael an easier time getting Jocelyn inside. Again, she seemed frozen in place, and Michael took matters into his own hands. He tucked her up into his arms again, ducking as he rushed away from the spinning rotors.

He climbed the stairs where he encountered Miss Tessa waiting for them. Now that he'd accomplished his goal to bring her home, he felt at a loss for what to do next. Luckily, his trusty chef already had a plan in place.

"Take her beside the fireplace. Carlos called ahead to warn me of her condition. Don't worry, Michael. We'll get her right as rain again in no time."

The butler held the door open while Michael shifted sideways to fit the two of them through the narrower opening safely. He saw the concerned looks on the staff's faces as he passed them by on the way to the fireplace. When he reached the roaring blaze, he bent to put her down onto the couch only to discover she clung to him like a burr in a dog's fur.

Rather than disturb her further, he twisted around until he could seat himself and settle her slight frame across his lap. He would have reveled in this position at any other time, but not today. Jocelyn's body and mind had suffered one tragedy too many in just as many days. This poor girl could hardly catch a break.

Miss Tessa brought warm towels and a bowl of steaming water. She kneeled in front of them both and began wiping Jocelyn's face clean as if she were a little child. Jocelyn didn't even seem to notice but kept her eyes closed and rested her head against Michael's chest.

Michael wished he could trade places with Tessa. He wanted to be the one to wash away the pain of Jocelyn's trauma, but he had to content himself with holding her tightly to him and remaining calm for them both. The heat from Jocelyn's body, combined with the fire, made Michael drowsy, but he refused to fall asleep.

"We should probably get her upstairs and into a bath," Tessa suggested in hushed tones.

Shaking his head, Michael answered, "I don't think she'd let me go, and I seriously doubt she'd want me to undress her." His hand rubbed across her back, wishing he could do just that but knowing it would be wrong. Especially considering she'd run away from the idea of marrying him.

"Why is she barefoot? What happened to her shoes?" Tessa asked as she wrung out the cloth to wipe off the mud from her feet.

"I can only guess she had an encounter with the swamp. She did say the swamp ate them." Michael chuckled with the remembrance of how she'd said it so seriously while they were out in the woods.

"Well, if that's the case, then she's lucky she didn't encounter an alligator. Poor girl. Why was she out there all alone anyway?" Tessa looked up to her employer as she rinsed off the towel again.

The fire's crackling and the trickling water in the basin were the only sounds in the room as Michael thought about how to answer that question without sounding completely absurd.

Michael answered quietly, letting out a long sigh, "We had a little misunderstanding."

At the end of his comment, Jocelyn flinched. Immediately, Michael's attention riveted to her. He hoped this meant the beginning of her coming back around to her senses. Unfortunately, she remained still and silent.

Tessa resumed her ministrations, tsking her tongue as she encountered scratches across the bottoms of Jocelyn's feet.

"From the looks of this, I'd say it was more than a *little* misunderstanding."

Her comment was under her breath and not one that Michael wanted to encourage. He already felt guilty enough without adding the cook's disappointment on top of it. He loved Tessa like family, but he had to remind himself that she was only the hired help.

Regrettably, that shift in thought only spread on another layer of remorse for minimizing her position in his life based solely on her employment. His grandma would have smacked him for such disrespect.

JOCELYN

It almost felt like she was coming out of a deep trance, but she didn't know when it had begun. She could hear a strong, steady heartbeat under her ear and the snapping of wood burning behind her. Other than those two touchpoints, she didn't have a clue where she was or how she got there.

Focus on what you know, she told herself sternly. This wilting flower act simply served to stir up her anger. She needed to get herself pulled back together. Little by little, she took stock of her body parts, all of which seemed normal except her feet had areas that were stinging strangely.

Finally, she opened her eyes and realized the heartbeat belonged to none other than Michael. She would never have imagined finding herself in this position, especially as she noticed he had her cradled on his lap with his arms around her as well.

Then it all hit her at once. The proposal. Her anger. Running away and getting lost in the dark. The animal coming to attack her. No, wait, it hadn't been an animal after all; it was Michael.

He'd come to find her and take her back to his house. She had her knight in shining armor, after all. As hard as it was to admit, she wanted it that way. Knowing he cared enough to come and find her, although she had no recollection of actually getting back.

She pushed herself away from him with her hand flat on his chest until she sat up straight. Looking into Michael's eyes, she saw a fleeting look before concern overrode whatever he had going on in his head. Swinging her feet over, she made to leave his lap, but his hands moved to her waist and kept her immobilized.

"Give yourself a minute to get oriented," he said.

Hope flared inside Jocelyn's heart, thinking he didn't want her to move, but then she immediately realized that wasn't the case.

He must have had plenty of time to reconsider his marriage proposal while she'd been out of it.

Well, she reasoned to herself, *I didn't want any part of it.*

Even the lie hurt her heart. She wanted to say yes to him more than anything, but her rational side told her he was still a veritable stranger. "I'm fine," she lied. She needed to get some distance between them until she could get her heartstrings under control again.

Miss Tessa chose that moment to make an entrance into the room. Jocelyn wondered if the woman had been listening just outside the room for her to wake up because she came bearing a cup of hot cocoa.

"I thought you might need something warm with sugar to boost your system from your shock," she said, handing it carefully to Jocelyn. Once her hands were free, she pointed down to Jocelyn's feet and asked, "How are they feeling?"

Jocelyn cradled the mug between her hands, bringing it up close under her nose so she could inhale the warmth and enjoy the chocolaty smell at the same time. Her nose wrinkled at Miss Tessa's remark and had to answer, "They sting quite a bit." Only then did some things strike her as odd. She was clean.

Eyes widening in alarm, she asked, "How long was I out, and how did I get clean?"

Tessa nodded to the cocoa and said, "Drink. It won't help until it gets inside you. As to your cleanliness, I towel-washed you while Michael held you right there," pointing to where Michael remained silent while taking in every detail.

Obediently, Jocelyn blew across the surface of the liquid before slurping in enough to swallow. This must have been the same recipe Michael had used; it tasted amazing. "Thank you, Miss Tess." She held up the cup and lifted one foot slightly before adding, "For both."

Looking over at Michael, she decided to bring up the elephant in the room. "We need to talk," she said pointedly. It might have been her imagination, but she could have sworn she saw him flinch. She couldn't blame him, not after how she stormed off before. But he wouldn't know that she'd had plenty of time to think things over while she'd wandered through the woods. It wouldn't hurt for her to hear him out.

CHAPTER 18

MICHAEL

Michael noticed Miss Tessa beat a hasty retreat at Jocelyn's simple statement. He wished he could follow along with her. Although, that wasn't his style. His father always told him to meet things head-on, and he agreed wholeheartedly.

"Right. About earlier, I'm sorry for practically pouncing on you with that stupid stunt." He could see he had her attention now, so he moved on to the negotiations he'd been rehearsing in his mind for the past hour while she slept.

"I've contacted my attorney to work out a substantial settlement—" Michael started.

Jocelyn's brows furrowed, and she held out one hand to get his attention. "Wait! If this is about me getting hurt on your property, then you should know I have no intention of suing you or anything. That's not my style."

Michael waved his hand dismissively. Holding her gaze with his steady one, he added, "No; this is for our marriage."

Jocelyn had started to take a sip of her cocoa as he spoke. Watching her sputter and choke while trying not to spill the contents of her cup, he realized his comment must have come across wrong. Finally, she managed to squeak out, "Excuse me? Am I missing something? When did we agree to get married?"

"When we were sitting under the tree. Remember? You said you'd help me however you could. I just thought—"

"You thought totally wrong. What would ever give you the impression we should get married?" Not finding a table close enough, Jocelyn leaned forward and set the mug on the floor.

Scooting to the edge of the couch, Michael rested his elbows on his knees as he shifted to get closer to her. Right now, the stiffness in her body made her nearly impossible to read, and he needed more information if he planned to make this deal work out. "After what you and my grandma were talking about, I just assumed she'd talked to you about my dilemma."

Jocelyn humorlessly chuckled as she shook her head, looking at him for all the world like he was a mistaken child. "We didn't discuss anything. She just started going on about us getting married like it was a done deal. I simply assumed it was part of her dementia. Are you saying she was serious?"

Michael nodded.

"I think you should start from the beginning because now I'm really confused."

Spending the next couple of minutes talking, Michael told her the bare bones of the problem. The exact details were less important than the conclusion he'd come to. He ended with, "So, you've seen first-hand how lively she got just at the idea of the two of us together."

He held up his hand to forestall her objection when he saw her draw in a breath. He continued, "If you agreed, then I'd make sure you and your family never wanted for anything. I wouldn't think to force you to stay with me if I made you miserable. We could get an amicable divorce, and I'd still make sure you had everything we agree to in our contract."

This time Jocelyn didn't stay seated. Jumping up from the chair, she began pacing in front of the fireplace. Michael had no idea what she was thinking, and it drove him crazy. She had to see this was the best solution for everyone involved.

Suddenly, she turned, hands fisted on her hips as she said, "So you're proposing we dupe your old and possibly senile grandmother into thinking we're a happy couple so you can save this?" She threw her arms wide to encompass everything around her.

But she wasn't done yet. Her voice rose another octave as she asked, "Do you honestly think I can be bought so easily? Are you really that depraved? Besides, what's wrong with turning this property into a wildlife refuge? It practically is already."

Michael couldn't stay seated with her hovering over him. It made him feel vulnerable. His anger began to rise, but he carefully tamped it down with his years of practice around his father. "There's absolutely nothing wrong with that plan. But—this is the only place that's ever felt like home to me, and I'd hate to lose it over a technicality."

"That's not good enough," Jocelyn shot out.

"I wasn't finished. What I was going to add was that I'd do anything to give my grandma a reason to keep living." Michael's shoulders slumped in defeat, and his voice lowered to almost a whisper as he added, "Even if that means I have to do the one thing I always swore I'd never do."

"I know you love your grandma, but there's got to be some way to reason with her. Doesn't she want you to be happy?" Jocelyn moved forward.

Michael shook his head and cried out, "Don't you think I already tried that angle. She won't budge. She's a stubborn woman once she sets her mind on something."

"Hmm. I'm starting to see it's a family trait." Jocelyn crossed her arms. "What did you mean you swore yourself off of marriage? Or was that just a figure of speech?"

Chuckling with genuine humor, he shook his head ruefully and said, "No. It was a real pact with my college friends."

"Seriously? Who does that outside of the movies?" Jocelyn seemed to wilt into the chair as she waited for him to answer.

Suddenly consumed with concern, Michael asked, "Are your feet hurting badly?"

"They've definitely been better. Don't change the subject. Tell me about this pact." She stretched out her legs so only her heels touched the hardwood floor.

"I could have Miss Tessa get something to make you more comfortable," he said, taking one step toward the kitchens.

Shaking her head until her hair swirled into her face, she pointed to the couch and said, "Sit down and start talking. I need to know everything before I can make an educated decision."

With alacrity, Michael dropped onto the couch. She practically admitted she was going to marry him. He simply had to come up with enough compelling reasons to keep her interested in the prospect. "As I said before, my buddies and I became friends in college. The six of us shared something unique in common."

Seeing Jocelyn raise her eyebrows in question, he added, "We all came from billionaire families. It was hard for us to trust anyone who came into our circle. I know it sounds snooty, but it's a real thing. You have no idea how many people just wanted to hang out with us so we could buy them things. It's disgusting."

Jocelyn snorted inelegantly and stated, "So you made a pact back in college that none of you would ever get married."

"Oh, it gets worse. Being foolish college kids on trust funds, we decided to up the ante."

Michael heard Jocelyn groan. He kept going, "The first one to get married would have to pay a million dollars to the rest of us. Likewise, the last one to get married would also have to pay out a million dollars to all of the others."

"Good grief! I can't tell if you boys were stubborn or just plain stupid! How's that working out for everyone? Are they all still single?

Michael shook his head and answered, "Two of them just got married."

"Let me guess – you don't want to be last and lose five million dollars. And that's where I come in. I see." Jocelyn crossed her arms again, her expression hardening as she came to that conclusion.

Michael sliced his hand down through the air dismissively. His voice rose as he exclaimed, "I could care less about that stupid bet and the money. I want to keep my grandma alive. You wanted to know the story, but it has absolutely no bearing on this discussion other than to say I never had any intention to marry. The pact simply made it easier to keep my mind set against it, but only as a joke among my friends."

"You need to get better friends." Jocelyn's voice dripped with sarcasm, and she rolled her eyes.

"Hey, we were young and arrogant. Will you help me with my grandma? Besides, she's already approved of you," Michael finished with what he believed was his final and most vital point.

JOCELYN

Is this guy serious right now?

She didn't honestly know his grandmother from any other stranger, so that argument didn't factor into her equation.

But she'd told herself she wouldn't jump to conclusions concerning Michael. The soreness of her feet could attest to the foolishness of impulsive thinking.

Watching him thoughtfully for several seconds, she decided he was dead serious about this whole crazy scheme. What would he do if she said yes? Heck, knowing him, he'd have a minister pop out of the closet and marry them on the spot. Or maybe Miss Tessa was already ordained and could do it herself.

A chuckle escaped unbidden from her lips until it ended with a sigh of resignation. "I want to meet with your grandma again."

Immediately, Michael lifted his wrist and checked the time.

"Jeez, Michael; not tonight! I'm not making any decisions of this magnitude after the past couple of days I've had."

"Right, right. I completely understand." He swiftly glanced around the room, searching for who-knew-what. "Did you want to spend the night here? Or do you want me to have Carlos get the helicopter ready to fly us back to my place tonight?"

"Right, your place. I'd forgotten that my apartment is, uh, uninhabitable right now," Jocelyn mumbled under her breath. Her life had gone off track lately. She sincerely hoped this wasn't becoming her new normal; she might not survive very long if that were the case. Clearing her throat as she came to a decision, she said, "We should stay here tonight."

Her inner monologue wouldn't slow down.

Since this could quite possibly be my new home, I should see what it's like at all hours. Besides, if it's haunted, all bets are off.

Leaving her alone in the luxurious guest bedroom, Jocelyn crossed the room to flop inelegantly onto the bed. How had she found herself in this position? Could she really be considering Michael's proposal?

The promise of money almost felt insulting, like he thought he could buy her love or loyalty. Besides, what would her parents say about this sudden change in her life? She pulled her arm up to cover her face like she used to do as a child when she had an important decision to make. Even through her mental turmoil, she didn't remember falling asleep, but her body obviously needed the healing reprieve.

CHAPTER 19

MICHAEL

Michael had everything arranged, but he still didn't know what Jocelyn had planned. He considered speaking with her about some ground rules where his grandma was concerned, but he hesitated. Would she consider his grandma's health when she spoke with her? He believed she would, based solely on the type of person she was. But still, was it worth the risk?

Gnawing on the inside of his cheek, he finally decided to say something. After all, she'd had time to think during the helicopter ride back to his car. Glancing over to her as he gripped the steering wheel tighter, he said, "About my grandma—"

Jocelyn cut him off. "You don't need to worry. I won't say anything to upset her. I promise."

"I didn't think you would, but I had to be sure. I'd do anything to protect her."

"I know." Jocelyn turned to face the window.

Michael still didn't have an answer from her, but at least he knew she'd be careful. The thoughts racing through his head didn't reassure him. Finally, he felt he had to say what was on his mind. "Is it really so terrible to consider marrying me?"

She turned to face him with a startled expression, and she blurted. "What? No." She clamped her mouth shut and turned back to the scenery outside the window. "The part which frustrates me the most is that you think you need to pay me to be with you. Or maybe worse, that you think I can be bought. Do you think so little of me?"

Michael couldn't believe that was all she got out of his proposal. After all, she was the one who ran when he proposed. Needing to set the record straight, he swerved the car over to the emergency lane on the side of the highway and slammed on the brakes.

"What's wrong? Is the car on fire or something?" Jocelyn looked around, her eyes wide with alarm.

"No, Jocelyn, we need to straighten out your thinking."

Instantly, her expression turned angry, and her arms crossed over her belly. "My thinking? It was your idea—"

"Only after you literally ran away from my proposal. I figured I must repulse you and hoped to offer you some incentive to be with me. I wanted to give you options in life."

"No, you wanted to bribe me into—"

"Stop it, Jocelyn. Even though you try to deny it, I'm trying to do the right thing here. How can you not see that?" His voice broke on the last sentence. Turning to face forward, he hoped she wouldn't think him weak. He'd always cultivated a persona of always having the answers, but he couldn't fix this.

JOCELYN

Jocelyn could have kicked herself for jumping to conclusions with him again. How many times could she fall into that habit with him? She had to say something to make things right again.

"Michael, the truth is," she began but faltered when Michael turned to look at her. His eyes held a sadness so deep that it almost crushed her soul. "I haven't always had charitable thoughts concerning you." There that was the most amicable way she could say it.

Pain washed over his eyes, followed instantly by confusion. "Why? Other than our occasional professional conversations, you didn't even know me until a few days ago." Michael turned his body to face her fully.

Gulping, Jocelyn knew she'd started this topic, and she had to follow through. Letting out a long sigh, she said, "I know your type. You're as handsome as hell, and you know it, you've got too much money to burn, and your ego is the size of Texas.

"Besides, I've heard your phone calls while you're waiting for your paperwork. You're the kind of guy I vowed to stop when I went into my line of work. Should I go on? Or do you get my point?" Jocelyn dumped everything she had on him; now, she waited to see how he'd respond.

"Wow. That was a long list of problems. I can't do much about some of those things, like my looks. I guess I could go around with a sour expression and try to repulse people with my grumpy behavior."

Jocelyn laughed. "Stop it, Michael. You're avoiding the bigger problems, and you know it." How could he get her to laugh even when she wanted to be stern with him?

"Fine, I'll try to be serious. Those phone calls you overheard were with my college friends."

"I told you they were a bad influence."

"Nah, it's just the way guys talk with each other. You know, always trying to one-up the other. Anyway, take a look at the transactions I've done. None of them took advantage of the people. Their properties would always have a lower value until I re-imagined the land use to something more profitable. Everyone walks away from my deals as a winner. I don't believe in taking advantage of people, unlike—"

He stopped talking to clear his throat.

"Can we try to have complete honesty with one another?" Jocelyn pressed.

Rubbing a hand across his face, Michael finally nodded. "I was going to say, my father. He doesn't have many scruples where business is concerned. As long as it's legal, he considers it fair game." Raising one of his eyebrows, he added, "He's the kind of guy you went into business to stop. Not me."

Jocelyn felt properly chastised. Now that she'd heard his side of the story, she knew he spoke the truth. With her long-time resentment toward him, she blinded herself to what he pointed out to her just now. His deals were more than fair for everyone. Her mind fabricated complaints against him simply to reinforce her faulty opinion.

Going against her rational brain, she said, "Fine."

"Fine, what? Please expand on that because I don't want to put my foot in my mouth yet again."

"Fine, as in I agree to marry you for your grandma's health."

Michael's countenance seemed to light up the interior of the car. The smile which spread across his face made her lips turn up in response to his childlike happiness.

Without any warning, Michael reached across the car and put his hands on either side of her face. He drew her close and placed a kiss so gentle on her lips that it almost felt like butterfly wings. His lips trembled. Could he feel the same from her?

Leaning into him, she pressed her lips harder against his. She wanted to make sure he remembered their first kiss well. He turned up the intensity by curling his fingers into her hair and letting out a small groan before pulling away a fraction of an inch.

"Thank you," he whispered, his breath tickling her already sensitive lips.

"You didn't let me finish," Jocelyn said seriously. When Michael pulled away, she wished she'd kept her mouth shut.

"Lay it on me," he offered.

"I won't take a cent from you. Not under any circumstances. And, heaven forbid, if your grandma should die before we get married, we'll have to discuss other arrangements. Can you agree to that?" Jocelyn bit her bottom lip, wishing it were Michael doing it instead.

"Fine." He held out his hand to seal the deal.

Looking down at it, she wondered if she should reconsider, but her heart told her something else. Before she could overthink it any more, she took hold of his hand, curling her fingers around his broad palm. As she'd anticipated, she felt his electricity coursing through her skin. "Do you feel that, or is it just me?"

"The static shock? Is that what you're talking about?" he asked.

"It happens every time you touch me. I don't think it's static."

"Hmm. Interesting." Michael cleared his throat again and asked, "Are you ready to go see grandma?"

"Absolutely. For the record, I'm glad we took this opportunity to talk right now."

"Me, too." Michael put the car in gear and turned on the signal to merge back into traffic. When an opening came, smaller than Jocelyn would have chosen, Michael hit the accelerator, and the car immediately shot into the stream of traffic without missing a beat.

Jocelyn still thought it almost magical that an electric car could be so powerful while remaining silent. The longer she rode in the car, the more she enjoyed it. Maybe she should tell Michael she would accept the car after all. Thinking better of it, she kept her mouth shut. She didn't want his money or what he could buy with it.

Michael turned up the radio. Jocelyn observed him from her peripheral vision. Was he thinking about what just happened between them? Was he regretting that she agreed to marry him? Or maybe he wasn't thinking about her at all.

"I love this song!" Jocelyn exclaimed, reaching over to turn up the sound even more.

Listening for a few seconds, Michael smiled when he heard Becky Easton's latest song playing. He opened his mouth as if he would say something but closed it.

They arrived at the care facility. After opening her door, Michael reached over and took her hand, twining his fingers with hers. She liked how it felt, but she noticed the dirty looks and glares from the female staff in the lobby.

She supposed she'd have to get used to it since she agreed to stay with Michael. All these changes from the past few days made her head spin. Her parents didn't even know about the car accident, let alone all the other calamities.

"I guess I'm going to have to take you home to meet my parents," Jocelyn said as she leaned closer to Michael when they reached the long hallway to the patients' rooms.

Michael's eyes widened, but the upward quirk of his mouth spoke something different. "This is getting serious, I guess."

Using her free hand, she smacked him playfully on the arm. "There's no way I'd get married and not invite my parents. Besides, they'd know something was up if they never even heard about you, and suddenly we got hitched."

Micheal kept looking straight ahead, but his lips curved up just slightly. "True. They'd probably think you were pregnant and forced to marry this ogre. Then they'd hate me for sure."

"Oh, you," she scoffed at his not-so-off-the-mark joke.

He stopped in front of the door with his hand resting on the knob. Michael's gaze held hers with an intensity she didn't understand. "Here we are. Are you ready?"

"You're making me nervous. Besides, she might not even remember who I am," Jocelyn said, mostly trying to convince her racing heart to calm down.

Michael knocked and opened the door. He held it open for her to enter first. Immediately, her hopes for anonymity were dashed.

"Josie and Michael!" Evelyn threw her legs off the side of the bed and grabbed up her robe from beside her. With a swirl of silk, she donned the robe. Her voice sounded clear and bright as she said, "Oh, I've worked out so many details for your wedding. Come and sit so we can discuss it."

Leaning in close so only Jocelyn could hear, Michael said, "It's a good thing you said yes." Then in a louder voice, he said, "You're in good spirits this morning, Grandma."

"It's certainly not because of this place. Did you know they almost drew all my blood out yesterday for the new rounds of tests you had ordered? But seriously, it's because of you, dear Mikey. You've given me so much joy by bringing Josie into our family. Come, sit. Sit." She pulled a notebook out from the bedside table and moved across the room with the speed and agility of a youngster.

Jocelyn cringed at the lie they were perpetuating, but she had to admit Evelyn looked much healthier today than she did the day before. Michael must have been correct in assuming that his grandma just needed something to live for.

How could she possibly deny the evidence right in front of her?

Would she go to the same lengths to save her parents? It didn't take long for her to conclude she would. Saving their lives would justify her sacrifice. Her thoughts jolted to a halt when she heard Evelyn speak.

"I think you should get married at the plantation house in June. It's the perfect month where everything's still green and in bloom, but it's not too hot yet."

"June? As in next year?" Jocelyn blurted.

Evelyn patted her hand and chuckled. "No, my dear. I wouldn't want to keep you from your happily ever after with Mikey. I'm talking about next month."

"Next month!" Jocelyn turned to Michael, eyes wide with fright and hoping he'd step in to help. This was moving way too fast, making her want to bolt.

Michael reached over and grabbed Jocelyn's hand. Maybe he could tell she wanted to bolt and decided to hold her in place. He gave her a reassuring squeeze before saying, "Grandma, there's no rush. We don't mind waiting so we can get all the details ironed out."

She tsked her tongue dismissively. "Don't be silly, Mikey. We've got enough money to make it happen tomorrow if we put our minds to it. No, a month is plenty of time for what I have in mind."

She turned away from Michael to address Jocelyn. Flipping through the pages of her notebook, she tapped her finger on a section and said to her, "What kinds of flowers would you like in your bouquet?"

"Um, I'm kind of partial to magnolias," Jocelyn replied.

Evelyn pounced on the suggestion and added, "Oh, they do smell delightful. Did Mikey take you out to the magnolia grove on the plantation yet?" When Jocelyn shook her head, she tsked her tongue again and gave Michael a disgusted look for the oversight.

Jocelyn instantly defended Michael, "It's not his fault, Evie. We haven't had much of a chance to explore."

"Well, I guess that's true. At least you'll have the rest of your lives to explore the property. So, I was thinking we could—"

Jocelyn couldn't believe all of the details Evelyn had already planned in just the last twenty-four hours. It almost made her head spin. Obviously, Evelyn wanted this wedding more than anything else in her life. Michael was right.

How could Jocelyn possibly deny a sweet, old lady her most desired dream?

CHAPTER 20
JOCELYN

"Are you ready for this?" Jocelyn asked Michael for the third time. She looked more nervous than he felt. Her nerves were beginning to cause him to think he had something to worry about after all.

"Absolutely. But there's something we need to take care of before we go inside," Michael answered, trying to make his voice sound more confident than he felt.

"What's that?" Jocelyn asked, her eyes immediately searching the car for something she might have missed.

Michael reached into his coat pocket, pulled out the small, black velvet box, and held it out toward her. He cracked open the lid and asked, "Will you marry me?"

"Oh, Michael! That's—" she started while staring wide-eyed at the three-carat diamond solitaire set in platinum. "Stunning."

"Well?" Michael prompted as he remained in his awkward position.

"What?" She pulled her eyes away from the sparkly diamond to look up at him.

"Will you marry me?" he asked again, a grin spreading across his lips until even his eyes crinkled at the corners with his mirth.

Her parents came out of their condominium before she opened her mouth to answer. Michael could instantly tell they were her parents since she vaguely resembled her father, but she was the spitting image of her mother. He also noticed that her mother spotted the ring and knew what was happening based on her hand covering her mouth.

"Your mom just spotted us. You better answer before she gets to the car, or I may never hear you say it."

"Yes, Michael. Yes!"

She threw her arms around his neck and planted a kiss right on his lips. Her exuberance surprised him, and he wondered if she'd planned this for her parents' benefit. Rather than dwell on that possibility, he leaned into the kiss, intensifying it for only a moment before pulling away.

He took the ring from the box and drew her left hand toward him. His fingers slightly shook as he passed the engagement ring over her knuckle until it rested in place. It fit perfectly. His heart skipped a beat as he realized this moment probably meant more to him than it did to her.

The next few minutes consisted of squealing, hugging, and general commotion until Jocelyn's mother got a hold of herself long enough for Michael to be properly introduced to her parents. Michael held out his hand to Ron and said, "It's a pleasure to meet you, sir." The two men appraised one another while keeping their grips firm.

Kathy didn't bother acknowledging his hand when he held it out to her. Instead, she flung herself against him, throwing her arms up around his neck and planting a firm kiss on his cheek. She pulled away and spoke to Jocelyn, "He's a handsome one. No wonder you've kept him all to yourself."

Ron seemed to have some sense of decorum because he cleared his throat loudly and said, "We've kept them waiting outside long enough, dear. Let's invite them inside already."

Michael smiled at his practical manner. Ron didn't tell his wife she was being rude, yet he still made his intentions clear. His own father would have had some scathing remark for his mother had it been his family.

The inside of their house gave off a similar vibe to Jocelyn's, obviously, without the destruction of the robbery. Since this was all their property money could afford, he could fully appreciate Jocelyn's desire to prevent unscrupulous real estate investors. More than anything, he wished he could help them financially, but he had to bide his time.

Kathy returned from the kitchen with glasses of iced sweet tea. She smiled warmly at Michael and said, "Do you know, you're the first boy Josie has brought home since high school. And now you're engaged. How did this happen? Where did you meet? How long have you been dating?" She turned away from Michael. Facing Jocelyn, she asked, "And how come this is the first time we've heard about Michael?"

Jocelyn squeezed Michael's knee, leaning in close to him, and said, "I tried to warn you." Turning to her mother, she said, "You know exactly why I don't talk about my male friends. You don't give me a moment's peace, and you're always pushing to have grandchildren."

Ron chuckled. "She's got you there, honey!"

Kathy glared at her husband before turning her attention back to Michael. It appeared he wasn't about to be let off the hook anytime soon.

"We met at Josie's work. She's been doing the paperwork for my real estate deals for quite a while now. I've always appreciated her skill at her job."

"Yes, she's quite brilliant, our girl," Kathy beamed.

"We've had a bit of time getting to know one another, and, as you saw outside, I decided I wanted to spend the rest of my life with her. She's just perfect, and I want her to be my wife."

Michael shifted his gaze to Ron and said, "I'm sorry I didn't ask your permission first. I'm pretty old-fashioned about most things, but the opportunity felt right. May I have your blessing to marry your amazing daughter?"

Ron opened his mouth to answer, but Kathy beat him to it as she exclaimed, "Of course he does! Right, honey?"

Raising his eyebrows in resignation for her enthusiasm, Ron nodded and answered, "Yes, Michael. Welcome to the family."

Kathy squealed again, reaching over to clasp one of Michael's hands and one of Jocelyn's. She squeezed them and exclaimed, "So when are you going to start a family?"

"Jeez, Mom. Give it a rest already," Jocelyn cried out in frustration.

Michael leaned over and planted a kiss on Jocelyn's cheek. Staying close, Michael answered, "We'll do our best to try to accommodate."

He grinned as he watched the red blush rise from her neck up to her cheeks. She looked so cute when she was flustered.

How could he resist when her mom gave him the perfect opening?

Kathy beamed with his answer. Giving his hand another squeeze, she asked, "So, have you thought about dates or venues?"

Michael nodded, bracing himself for the backlash. "Yes. Next month at my family's plantation."

"Next month!" Kathy's eyes registered alarm, and she turned to Jocelyn and said, "That hardly gives us any time to get ready. I've got so many ideas!"

"Well, Mom, you'll have to get in line behind Michael's grandma. She's already got the caterers on speed dial."

"Oh, how fun! We can work on it together. You'll have to give me her phone number, and we can start collaborating. Although it would've been nice to have more notice." Kathy gave her daughter an accusatory look.

Thinking a change of subject was in order, Jocelyn immediately replied, "Yes, it would've been nice to know you'd decided to start selling your paintings. When did that happen?"

Waving offhandedly, she replied, "Oh, nobody's ever going to want to buy that. Besides, it's in a nursing home or something. How on earth did you find out about it?"

Jocelyn grinned and answered, "Michael's grandma is staying in that care facility. Otherwise, I'd never have known you started showing your art. I'm proud of you, Mom."

Driving back to Atlanta, Jocelyn's mind kept going over the visit with her parents. It went much easier than she ever would have dreamed possible. Her mother was so excited to see her married; she didn't even give Michael the third degree he deserved for the suddenness of their wedding. It almost freaked her out a little with how easy it all went.

Wanting to feel like some things were still normal, she turned to Michael and said, "I'd like to go to my apartment tonight if you don't mind." A strange expression flitted across his face, but he nodded readily enough, so she dismissed it.

Jocelyn's phone beeped with an incoming text message. What could her boss want from her? Opening the message, her cheeks warmed with anger. Slamming her phone back into her purse, she stared out her window with her mind seething.

"Is everything okay? You look upset." Michael spared several glances from driving to check on her.

"That was Mr. Bandy. He said I didn't need to come back to work since my performance hasn't been up to his standards lately. He said I could pick up my things and my final paycheck tomorrow." She looked over to Michael and saw the same anger sparking in his eyes.

"I'm sorry, Josie. I guess I'll have to find another title company to handle my business since I only trusted you to get my paperwork in order. He doesn't know just how much he's lost by letting you go.

"You don't need to worry about that job anyway. Besides, I think Mr. Bandy's a creep, and you're better off not being around him."

Jocelyn sighed. Her life seemed to be changing by the minute. First her car, then her house, and now her job—all gone. One by one, everything seemed to disappear. She could console herself with the fact she'd never have to endure being sexually harassed by her boss again.

Almost an hour later, Michael pulled over in front of the apartments into the same spot he had before. This time, Jocelyn waited for Michael to get her door without any argument. Without any invitation, their hands joined as they walked up the sidewalk to her place.

Michael's steps slowed down the closer they got to her front door. Jocelyn realized he must have had some hand in getting it repaired since a brand new door stood in place of the old, beat-up, broken one.

"You had my door fixed! Thank you, Michael." She pulled him down for a kiss on the cheek. "Were you trying to surprise me?"

"Um. We'll see," he answered noncommittally.

"Is something wrong," she asked, finally deciding not to let it drop unsaid this time.

Instead of answering, Michael gestured for her to unlock the door. She dug her key from her purse and pressed it into the lock. When the door swung in, her mouth dropped open in shock. Turning to Michael, she asked, "Did you do this?"

"Yes. I can explain," he started.

"Oh? You have an explanation as to why all of my stuff is now missing from my apartment?" She stomped through the empty living room and into the kitchen. Pulling a random drawer open and finding it empty, she whirled around and asked, "Where's all my stuff?"

"I had a team come in and pack it up for you. I figured..."

"What did you figure?" she asked, crossing her arms and advancing on him. Coming within a few inches of him, she asked, "That you could take my stuff and pack it away so you could keep me hostage?"

Michael threw his head back and laughed.

Hard.

Jocelyn stared at him, wondering why he could find this the least bit amusing. Her stuff was gone, and he had planned it. What if she hadn't agreed to marry him? What would he do then?

But she did agree. Now she didn't have to worry about her place anymore. His gesture actually took a huge burden from her mind. Once these positive thoughts began to roll in, she could see the humor in the situation.

A chuckle rose from deep within, erupting from her mouth. Before long, the two of them fell to the floor in a heap, both laughing uncontrollably.

"Oh, Lordy! I thought the ruffians had returned," Mrs. Abernathy announced from the open doorway.

Jocelyn saw her neighbor from across the hall, looking as disheveled as ever. For some reason, even her entrance caused her to laugh even harder. Now her cheeks and stomach began hurting.

She'd have to get control of herself before Mrs. Abernathy began spreading the word that she was on drugs or something. That lady positively loved to spread gossip, real or imagined.

"Oh, Mrs. Abernathy. I'm so glad I could see you one last time," Jocelyn said, chuckling a few more times but rising to her feet.

She offered a hand to help Michael up from the floor. Once they were standing, she pulled him with her toward the front door. "I wanted to share our amazing news with you." She held out her left hand to show her ring and said, "We're getting married! Michael's already arranged a new place to live until the ceremony. Isn't that amazing?"

Mrs. Abernathy leaned forward to inspect the ring. She nodded approvingly and looked over to Michael to say, "You did good, boy." She turned around and announced, "I'll be sure to let everyone know." The door slammed across the hall without a backward glance.

"I'm sure you will," Jocelyn muttered. Looking up at Michael, she said, "She loves to gossip. We just gave her enough juicy tidbits to last her the rest of the month." Looking around one last time, she said, "There's nothing here for me. Let's go home."

"I love the sound of that."

MICHAEL

Once they returned to the front gates, Michael became serious again. Even though the gate opened, he didn't begin to drive through. "I've got another surprise for you. Please don't get too excited before I explain."

"I promise to keep an open mind. Let's just get inside. It's almost time for Meow Meow to eat anyway."

Michael hesitated for seconds, then let the car roll up the driveway. Jocelyn hardly noticed the yard passing by outside, but she did see someone's car parked out front.

"Do we have a visitor?" she asked, pointing to the car.

Pulling up behind the car, he parked. "No. That's my surprise for you."

Jocelyn's eyes began to fill with tears.

Michael had no idea how to help her now. As if in slow motion, she opened her car door and got out of the Tesla. Faster than he thought possible, she began circling the car and then running over to him.

Giving him a hug which all but kept him from breathing, she said, "How did you know this was my dream car?"

"Your dream? I didn't. I just thought you enjoyed the Tesla, but you didn't want something so expensive. I imagined what you would buy, and I thought of this. Do you really like it?"

"Like it? No, I love it! Do you know this was the exact car I've been saving for over the last two years?" She shook her head in disbelief.

"Well, then, I'm glad I picked it out for you. Since that gift went so well, then maybe you'll like the flight lessons I arranged for you."

Jocelyn's face turned positively radiant with this latest news. "You're joking, right?"

"Nope. I arranged for you to get lessons from my friend, Richard. He owns an airplane manufacturing company, but he's also a flight instructor. He only takes special students, and he agreed to begin lessons with you next week."

Jocelyn squealed again and gave him another exuberant hug. He loved making her giddy; it tickled his heart to see her so happy. He wanted this for her every day of their lives together. "Let's go inside and feed Meow Meow. We can discuss the details over some hot cocoa." He took her hand, and they walked inside together.

Jocelyn stopped dead in her tracks as soon as they entered the house. Michael somehow managed yet another surprise in the form of new artwork prominently displayed in the foyer. "When did you do this?" she asked, pointing to her mother's painting.

"My assistant picked it up today. Your mother's very talented, and I knew you loved it. Do you like your surprise?" Michael seemed unsure of himself as he waited for her answer.

"I love it. Thank you!" she cried out, once again throwing her arms around his neck and planting a kiss firmly on his lips. The hot chocolate would have to wait a bit longer.

CHAPTER 21
(ONE MONTH LATER, WEDDING DAY) - JOCELYN

"Mom, Evie, and you outdid yourselves in putting this wedding together. I think everything is perfect!" Jocelyn said as she looked at her mother's reflection in the dressing room mirror. She watched her mom fuss with the tiara holding her veil, seeing the tears starting to fill her lower lashes.

"Please don't start crying, Mom. I'll ruin my makeup!"

"I can't help it. You look so amazing. I still can't believe all of this will be yours. This is almost like our old home, you know. Well, not the house, but the property. You've come full circle, and you look stunning." Kathy hugged her from behind, pressing her cheek against Jocelyn's.

"Yes. And don't forget that you and Dad get to move into Michael's beautiful city home. Everything is turning out just like a dream."

Jocelyn only felt a twinge of guilt that she had started to believe this marriage was real and not a financial agreement with a signed contract. More than anything, she wanted it all to be true, but she'd have to hope Michael would eventually see her as more than a business partner.

"I have to go check on a few last-minute details. Are you going to be okay until your father gets here?" Kathy asked.

"Sure, sure. Go do your thing. I'll be right here waiting." Turning, she put her hand over her mother's and said, "I love you, Mom. Thank you for all of this."

Kathy swooped down and kissed Jocelyn's cheek before turning and leaving the small room. Jocelyn returned her gaze to her reflection, seeing the sparkle in her eyes and wishing this day could be so much more. Determined to remain positive, she dabbed on a bit more pink lipstick and smacked her lips together.

The door opened behind her, and a man walked in. It wasn't her father. She turned in alarm and asked, "Can I help you with something?"

"It sure took that old bitty long enough to leave."

"Excuse me? I sure hope you aren't referring to my mother. Who are you?" Jocelyn stood up and whirled around to face this nasty stranger. He took two steps closer, and Jocelyn drew in a breath with recognition. "You're Michael's father."

"I'm glad to see he's told you about me. Unfortunately, he's shared nothing about you." With a scathing glance up her body and ending with her face, he added, "And now I can see why. You'll never be good enough for this family. I hoped you'd see that before this day came, but I see you might need more motivation to see the truth."

He thrust his hand out, which held a piece of paper. "Take it and leave. We don't want your kind of gold-digging trash in our family."

Automatically, Jocelyn's hand took the paper because it was polite to take a gift. Her eyes dropped from Theodore's scathing look to see he had given her a check. A million-dollar check to be more precise.

"That's what I thought," Theodore sneered. "You're only after my money. I'll be sure to let Michael know you've changed your mind. Good day, hussy." Theodore may have left the room, but his threatening presence lingered long after the door slammed shut.

Jocelyn's legs felt as though they'd turned to rubber. Unable to hold herself up any longer, she wilted into a puddle of fabric and tears right where she had stood. She didn't care about her makeup anymore; there wouldn't be a wedding, not after Theodore got done with Michael.

A wave of righteous anger stirred up in Jocelyn. She took the check and ripped it to shreds which she thrust out toward the door. "Keep your damned money!" she cried out before dropping her face into her hands and letting the tears flow.

"Honey? Are you okay? What's wrong, baby? Did someone hurt you?" Ron asked, immediately dropping to his knees next to his daughter.

"I think we should go home, Dad. I'm not welcome here." A fresh wave of remorse washed over her as her mind replayed the terrible tableau from only minutes before. She was a fraud, and Theodore's accusations truly hit home.

"Nonsense, honey. Michael sent me to find you. He's waiting for you at the altar. Come on. Let's get you freshened up, and you can see for yourself." Ron practically picked her slight frame up and manhandled her over to the dressing table. Picking up a tissue, he dabbed at her face. He grabbed a makeup brush and perused the powders on the table. "Which one of these goes with this brush?" he asked playfully.

Jocelyn couldn't help but laugh at her father's attempt to help. If it were left up to him, she'd end up looking like a clown. Taking the brush from his hand, she repaired the damage to her makeup.

She knew her father wouldn't mislead her. If he said Michael still wanted her, she would believe it until she heard differently from Michael's own lips.

"I'm ready," she announced and stood. She accepted the bouquet her father held out for her and then took her place next to him with her hand resting inside his elbow. "Thanks, Dad."

"You look beautiful, baby." He led the way to the waiting crowd.

The music started as soon as she appeared. Her eyes scanned the crowd for any sign of Theodore, but he was nowhere in sight. Leaning over to her father, she whispered, "Where's Michael's dad?"

"He left. He argued with Michael, and then he drove off in a huff. It was pretty poor taste if you ask me. This is supposed to be a happy occasion."

Jocelyn's fears waned, knowing that Theodore wasn't lurking anywhere to ruin this day for her. He'd done his best, but he didn't win. Her eyes finally spotted Michael where he stood next to the minister.

The smile on his face practically beamed, and her own probably mirrored it. This was the moment she'd always dreamed of having. Michael was her dream.

MICHAEL

Michael remembered to breathe deeply as he watched Jocelyn walk up the aisle to him. Of course, his father lied when he said she changed her mind. It was a good thing his father left, or he might consider rearranging his face for attempting to ruin his wedding day.

The next few minutes passed in a blur, but then Jocelyn stood directly in front of him. His hands held hers, and he stared into her bright and shining eyes. She'd been crying. Probably from his father's visit to her. Another grievance to add to his lengthy list against his father.

Jocelyn finished stating her vows, and now it was Michael's turn. The minister turned to him and said, "Michael Theodore Cavanaugh, repeat after me."

"Wait!" Michael announced, bringing a halt to the entire ceremony. "Jocelyn, I can't do this." Her eyes brimmed with tears before he got the following sentence out.

"I can't go through with this unless you can promise me that this will be forever. I'll give up everything, this property, all my money, everything because I love you more than anything, and I want this to be real or not happen at all. If you want to leave, I'll understand.

"Before you answer, know I'll still make sure you and your parents are financially set, so I want your decision to be from your heart, not from any feelings of guilt or obligation toward myself or my grandma."

A strange look crossed Jocelyn's face, and she asked, "Do you mean that? You actually love me?"

"Yes, Jocelyn. I love you, and I want to marry you for real. If I can't have that, I don't want to go through with this."

Jocelyn's face transformed from confused to radiant. She flew forward and kissed Michael right on the lips, her arms snaking around his neck. He only just managed to keep to his feet at her miraculous assault, but he responded in kind.

A second later, Michael reluctantly pulled away and asked, "Do you truly want to be my wife?"

"I DO!" she cried out, planting another kiss on his lips.

The crowd stood, many of them cheering or clapping at the happy ending. The minister cleared his throat beside them and said, "I now pronounce you husband and wife since you've already kissed the bride."

More laughter followed his statement, and Michael grabbed Jocelyn's hand and raised it with his in victory. Together they ran down the silk-covered aisle where the crowd showered them with dry rice.

Dancing would begin immediately, and Michael's surprise awaited. He could hardly contain his excitement, knowing Jocelyn would be beyond excited.

The crowd followed them to the barn's cool interior, which they transformed into a dancing venue fit for a fashion magazine. The white string lights twinkled overhead while the candles flickered on the beverage tables all around the room. The freshly lacquered floor made it appear as though they danced on water.

On the far side, a raised platform held the band. Michael kept Jocelyn's attention away from the entertainment until the guests crowded into the barn. As soon as he saw his grandma enter the room, he signaled the band. This was the dance he planned, their first dance to show her how much he wanted to shower her with surprises.

With the opening notes, Jocelyn's face lit up. "How did you know this was my favorite song? Although it's kind of a strange one for a wedding. Don't you think? Oh, I hope the cover band does a good job with it."

Michael pulled Jocelyn close, his grin matching hers. But he knew a secret that she would soon discover. This wasn't a cover band; it was Becky Easton herself singing a live version just for them. Just as Becky got to the chorus about the red, high-heeled shoe, Michael turned Jocelyn to face the stage.

He knew the exact moment when she saw the singer as her body stiffened. Leaning forward, he whispered, "Surprise."

"How?" she asked, her gaze never leaving the stage.

"I never told you that Becky is married to one of my college buddies. You know, the friends you told me I could do better without."

This time, Jocelyn turned around, her face flushing with excitement and embarrassment. "Michael, I didn't mean that. I can't believe Becky Easton is singing at my wedding. At our wedding!"

She flung her arms around his neck and planted a kiss on his lips. Pulling away, she said, "Thank you. You've made this day perfect, despite the short notice. I love you."

"I love you." He grinned and added, "When we're done with our dance, I'll take you over to meet Randy and Becky. You're going to love them."

"Oh, wow! I never imagined meeting her. What will I say?"

"You'll think of something." Michael lifted her arm and gave her a twirl before bringing her close again to sway to the rest of the song. Once the song finished, he slid his hand down her arm until his fingers intertwined with hers. He drew her close to the stage, noticing how she practically buzzed with excitement.

Becky turned away from thanking the band and came face-to-face with the bride and groom. "Michael!" she cried out, hopping off the stage and hugging him.

As soon as she let him go, she turned to Jocelyn and said, "I never thought I'd see the day when someone would steal Michael's heart. You must be amazing, Jocelyn. Oh, sorry, my name's Becky. I'm married to Randy Easton, your husband's friend from college."

Jocelyn gave Michael a significant look and said, "Michael was just telling me. Thank you so much for singing your song at our wedding. It's my absolute favorite. You must hear that a lot, though. I can't believe you're here. I feel so lucky."

"I'd do anything for Randy's friends. They're a great group of friends. Have you met them all yet?" Becky asked, her eyes shifting toward the crowd to find them.

"Not yet, but I'm sure I will before the day is out."

"Oh, I see Richard just over there. Let's go say hello."

Michael leaned closer and said, "He's going to be your flight instructor."

"Oh! Well, lead on then. This day is just full of surprises!"

Taking her hand, Michael never let go of it for the rest of the evening. After hours of dancing, cutting the cake, throwing the bouquet, and mingling with guests, they were pretty worn out and ready to call it an evening.

The crowds had considerably thinned before they made their escape back to the main house and out of the heat. They planned to change their clothes before leaving for their honeymoon. In anticipation of getting into more comfortable clothes, Michael had already unfastened his tie and the top button of his shirt as they walked through the front door.

They only made it to the foyer before Miss Tessa intercepted them. A severe expression covered her usually cheery face. She held a phone in her hand, shaking her head.

"What's wrong, Tessa?" Michael asked. Did something happen to his grandma? He just saw her enjoying the company of the last few guests.

"The police just called to say that your father was involved in a car crash. I'm so sorry, Michael. He didn't survive. They said he was already gone by the time they were on the scene."

Strangely enough, Michael didn't feel anything with Tessa's news.

Nothing.

Rather than ruin any more of this day with the man he called his father, he said, "Thank you, Tessa. Please tell my mother outside. My bride and I are going up to our room."

Michael shut their bedroom door by leaning back against it. His head rested on the hardwood as he breathed out a long sigh. Jocelyn pressed up against him, offering her physical support.

"Are you okay, Michael? I'm so sorry for your loss." She pressed her hands to his cheeks and forced him to look at her.

"Is it terrible to say that I'm glad he's gone? Do you know he tried to tell me you changed your mind and that you accepted money from him to leave? I didn't believe him for an instant and told him to leave. It serves him right that he'd crash his car after trying to pull a stunt like that on my wedding day."

"Michael, I did take a check from him when he came to my dressing room just before the ceremony. But I tore it up.

At first, I didn't know what he was giving me or who he was really, but then he made things all too clear. He called me a gold-digging hussy and that I didn't belong in *his* family. He said you changed your mind, and it about broke my heart."

"Is that why you looked like you'd been crying? That bastard! I'm glad he's dead, or I'd kill him myself!"

"Michael, please don't talk like that. It scares me." Jocelyn pulled her hands away, and she stepped back from him.

"I'm sorry, Josie. I don't ever want you to be afraid of me. I love you, and I'll spend the rest of my life proving it to you. Starting right now, Mrs. Cavanaugh!" He propelled himself forward and cradled Jocelyn in his arms, startling her into a playful squeal of delight.

Dropping a kiss onto her lips, he didn't come up for air until they both forgot all about any unpleasantness of the day.

CHAPTER 22
(Two Weeks Later) - Michael

"Oh, Mikey. My precious boy," his mom said to him, entreatingly reaching out her hands. The tears in her eyes looked genuine, but Michael knew better than to fall for her trick. She hadn't spoken his nickname since he stopped living with her at the age of ten.

This was the first time she'd come to see him since his father's death. He wondered how long it would take her to come crawling to him for something. She probably needed money for her country club dues since his father had left her only the house and a small pension. For the rest of his father's fortune, he willed to his favorite golf course.

His feet remained firmly planted, only his breathing quickening as his anger rose. "Mother, I'm not falling for your act. I'm too old to need a mother. Besides, I've got Grandma, who has always been more of a mother to me than you ever were." Michael crossed his arms; his steely eyes glared at her blatant attempt to coerce him to feel pity for her.

"You have no idea what I've gone through. Your father was a hard man to live with."

"Trust me; I know," Michael spat back. He endured enough verbal abuse from his father over the years to leave deep scars on his soul.

"I've always loved you, but I had to pretend not to so your father would leave you alone. Come, let's go talk with Evelyn. She knows the truth." She attempted to touch his arm, but Michael shifted away to avoid the contact. She flinched with the insult, but she turned and led the way out of the room.

As Michael stepped into the foyer to follow, the front door opened. Jocelyn's radiant smile froze on her lips as she felt the tension radiating from him. She raised an eyebrow at Michael's hardened look.

Hastily shutting the door, she came up beside him. "What's going on?" she whispered.

"Mother's trying to play me again. She says my grandma can corroborate her trumped-up tale." Michael put his arm around her waist and drew her close to his side.

He inhaled her scent, already feeling some tension releasing just from her presence. He needed to feel her next to him to draw strength from her calmness.

"Let's go then," she said, taking a step and forcing him to follow along.

By the time they got to the sunroom, Lena had already seated herself next to Evelyn on the wicker loveseat. With Meow Meow draped across Evelyn's lap, she stroked the cat with one hand and had her other arm across Lena's shoulders. She whispered something into her ear.

Michael already didn't trust this scene. His grandma had never lied to him, and he knew he could believe whatever she said, but this was getting close to his breaking point. "Grandma. Mother said you could tell me the truth in this matter."

"Sit down, Mikey. Josie, I'm glad you're here as well." She gestured for them to seat themselves across from the loveseat.

Michael pulled the chairs closer to one another to keep physical contact with Jocelyn. He drew in a shaky breath, fearing he already knew the truth and not wanting to admit any of it to himself.

Evelyn waited several seconds before saying, "Lena came to see me when you were almost ten years old. She begged me to take you into our house to raise because she feared your father would kill you."

"What? That's preposterous. I'm sure Mother was just having drunken hallucinations or something."

"Mikey, stop talking nonsense until you hear the whole story," Evelyn spoke sternly.

Even as an adult, Michael felt like a little child as she chastised him in front of his wife. He knew his grandma was right, which made it twice as bad. Clamping his mouth shut, he simply nodded for his grandma to continue.

"Your father was an extremely jealous man. He hated the fact that your mother loved you more than she could ever love him. He made her life a living hell until she sent you away to boarding school. She only consented because she thought you'd be safer at the school than you'd ever be at home with your father.

"You wouldn't remember this, but you had to be hospitalized for brain trauma when you were just a baby. The doctors were told that you fell down the stairs, but the truth was that your father shook you because you were crying in your crib. He said you were disturbing him as he was trying to watch a football game.

"Your mother walked in on the scene and beat your father until he let you go. He punched her before stalking out of the room, yelling, 'Keep that brat quiet!' She scooped up your unconscious body and took you to the hospital. She most likely saved your life that day."

Lena sniffed loudly and added, "I knew you'd never be safe after that. I learned that if I ignored you, then your father was happier. He had to believe that I didn't care for you to allow you to remain living in the house. Immediately, I hired a nanny to keep you busy and away from us. But my plan didn't work for very long.

"To cover up my pain, I started drinking. I hated every part of the lie we were living and that you were getting hurt because of him." She stopped to blow her nose.

Michael couldn't remain seated any longer. He jumped from his chair to pace. His sudden movement caused his mother to cry out in alarm. Only then did he realize the life of terror she'd been living. If only they'd told him about it, he could have helped her.

Finally, Michael stopped pacing and cried out, "Why didn't you leave him? You could've taken me, and we could've run away! You didn't have to abandon me and make me think you hated me all these years!"

"Michael!" Evelyn said.

Lena raised her hand and said, "No, Evelyn. He has a right to ask these questions. I know how much I've hurt him, and I want to help him understand."

She shifted her gaze up to Michael and said, "Your father threatened to kill you if I ever tried to leave him. I believed him because he was holding a knife to your neck as he said it. He made me promise on your life that I'd never leave him. I'd never put you at risk, so I agreed."

Michael's hand automatically moved to touch the scar on his neck – the one he'd never known how it had gotten there. Now he knew the truth, but it didn't stop the pain.

"When you kept calling home to say how much you hated boarding school, I knew I had to find another solution for you. I finally approached Evelyn and Ernest and confessed what was happening. They agreed to take you, love you, and keep you safe from Theodore."

Michael resumed his pacing. Suddenly he turned to his grandma and asked, "Remember that time when I was out playing in the forest until almost dark. That poacher said he thought I was a deer and shot me in the arm – was that really a poacher or someone my dad hired?"

Evelyn and Lena exchanged a meaningful look before Lena broke into another crying fit. It only lasted a few seconds before she shook her head. Although muffled through the tissue she held to dab her nose, she said, "I was late coming home from the country club. Your father thought I needed a reminder of his threat."

"It wasn't until your father died that I felt it was safe to tell you the truth. I couldn't risk having you confront him on the matter."

"It's true. I would've gone and punched him in the face for all the times he insulted you. I can't believe I didn't see any of this before," Michael's voice lowered until it was only a whisper at the end. It all made perfect sense now. His father tried to ruin everything for him because of his jealousy. It almost made him sick to think he was blood-related to a man that vile.

"I'm so sorry, Mom." Michael fell to his knees in front of his mother and buried his head in her lap. His arms looped around her waist, and the two of them cried. Nobody existed outside their circle of pain and healing.

The ice he held in his heart melted the instant he felt her arms wrap around him. She held him like she was going to break if the contact ended.

For the first time, he truly felt loved and wanted by her, yet he'd had it all along because of her sacrifice. He'd been blind and stupid with his anger, but that would end today.

His father could no longer taint his happiness.

EPILOGUE

(One Month Later) - Michael

"Are you sure?" Michael asked for the third time. He clutched the phone so hard that he thought he might crack the casing. But this news wasn't something to get wrong.

Jocelyn entered his office just as he hung up the phone. "Is something wrong?" she asked as soon as he saw his strange expression.

Not able to remain seated, Michael stood and crossed around his desk to stand in front of his wife. "I just got a call from the lab at Grandma's care facility. Do you remember that battery of tests that they wanted to run the day we told Grandma we were together?"

"Gosh, that was like eight or nine weeks ago now."

"Ten, actually. Well, the lab wanted to be thorough and ran all of the tests several times before they came back with their diagnosis. They assured me there's absolutely no chance they're mistaken this time."

"This time? I don't understand. What did they find? Is your grandma okay?" Jocelyn searched his face for trouble.

His thoughtful expression morphed into an exuberant smile as he announced, "Grandma doesn't have Parkinson's after all. They were wrong."

"How could they get that wrong? Doesn't she display all the signs?"

"Yes, which was why they came up with that diagnosis, especially given her age. But they discovered she has polycythemia. The symptoms are nearly identical to Parkinson's at the early stages, but the treatments are quite different."

"What does that mean for her now? Can she come home to live here again?" Jocelyn beamed with hope.

"Do you want her to? I promised you that we could live here, but if you want a place of our own, I will get you whatever you need." Michael meant every word he said, but he hoped they could stay there.

"She absolutely needs to come back here. This is her home first. I just hope she won't mind sharing it with us!"

"I love you! You've made me the happiest man all over again. I'll have Genevieve make the arrangements for her transport home as soon as possible." Michael turned away and called his personal assistant.

When he finished, he said, "Are you all set to go flying?"

"Yep. I was just coming to get you. We can postpone today's lessons if you want to see your grandma. It's fine with me."

"No, that's okay. I spoke with Grandma earlier, and she said she has lots to get squared away there, and she didn't have time for me until later today. You know how she can get when she sets her mind to something."

"Boy, don't I just. All I have to do is look at you, and I see reflections of her every day! Come on; we should get going if we want to be on time. Today will be easy now that we're already flying high on your amazing news."

Michael delayed them for a few minutes longer as he pulled his wife into his embrace. "Have I told you how much I love you today?"

"At least three times, but who's counting," she replied, grinning foolishly.

Everything he never knew he wanted was right in front of him. Even better, his grandma had many years left to live with them. Their lips joined together to show their perfect love for one another. Inhaling her vanilla-scented perfume, he knew this day would forever be imprinted in his mind as when his life became perfect.

"She's a natural pilot," Richard announced as they taxied up the runway. "I've had some good students before, but your wife's the best student and pilot I've ever had the pleasure to teach."

Michael beamed as he watched from the back seat of the small aircraft. He asked to do a fly-along, and Jocelyn agreed. From the moment they got to the airport, her casual demeanor changed to that of a professional pilot.

He watched in awe as she inspected the plane, filed their flight plan, spoke with the tower, and finally took off with him for the first time. He'd say he was flying with a seasoned professional if he didn't know better. Of course, he was probably biased, but Richard's praise only proved his instincts.

"Well, I have an amazing instructor," Jocelyn broke in, her cheeks flushing with the praise but continuing to keep focused until she parked the plane in front of their private hangar. After she shut down the engine, she unbuckled and twisted around in her seat to ask, "What did you think?"

"I loved it, and I love you!" Michael leaned forward to plant a sloppy kiss on her lips.

Richard made playful gagging sounds.

Michael chuckled and broke away. "Hey, Richard, don't knock it until you try it yourself. Speaking of, how's the wife hunt going for you?"

"Dude, you know marriage isn't even on my agenda. To be honest, when I heard you were getting hitched, I thought it was a prank. You were the least likely ever to get roped into it out of all of us." He glanced toward Jocelyn and added, "No disrespect intended. I think you two are perfect for each other. I just don't see the same thing happening for me."

Michael and Jocelyn looked at one another meaningfully before they both laughed uncontrollably. Michael recovered first. He planted his hand hard on Richard's shoulder and said, "Love strikes where you least expect it. Good luck, man!"

The End...For Now

Continue the series with *Plane Love*, Book 4 in

the Billionaire's Bet Romances.

CHAPTER 23
BONUS: FIRST CHAPTER OF PLANE LOVE

The scorching Texas sun beat down on Richard as he sat at the outdoor table, eagerly awaiting the arrival of his hickory slow-smoked beef short ribs drenched in mouthwatering sweet and spicy sauce.

The sizzling aroma teased his senses, momentarily distracting him from the whirlwind of emotions stirring inside.

Lillith's recent flirtations with the gym trainer had taken him on an unexpected journey down memory lane. He should be relieved she was directing her attention elsewhere.

Yet it still stung.

His phone chimed with an unread message, as if adding insult to injury, reminding him of the day he stumbled upon Lillith's deceitful texts to her friends.

He thanked his lucky stars for that accidental glimpse into her true intentions. It had been a wake-up call, revealing her intentions to marry him solely for his wealth, he might have been stuck with the gold-digger for life, or worse, for decades of alimony payments. The warning signs had been there all along, but he had brushed them aside under his father's enthusiastic approval of Lillith and her influential family.

Still, he hadn't quite let go of the crushing dagger-to-the-heart feeling, which dug a little deeper when he unexpectedly saw her in the gym. As if fate were toying with him, he had just finished his bench press, narrowly avoiding a disastrous accident over his chest.

Escaping unnoticed, he fled to the locker room, grabbed his gym bag, and slipped out of a side exit, wanting to avoid any confrontation with Lillith. He couldn't help but imagine the dramatic scene she would have caused had she spotted him.

Driving away from the gym, Richard couldn't help but wonder if Lillith had spotted his distinctive black Rolls Royce Phantom in the parking lot. The rarity of such a car in the area made it hard to miss. He contemplated his friend Markson's offer to buy it, thinking that maybe it was time for a change. Markson would probably jump at the chance if he mentioned it.

A new gym was definitely in order; he couldn't risk running into Lillith again. Her relentless calls had only ceased four months ago, probably because she found a new target. Good riddance, he thought, relieved to be free of her clutches.

But the day wasn't over yet, and his phone continued to pester him with notifications, the lock screen filled with unread messages until he flipped the phone over on the table.

Could this day get any worse?

As the server approached with his platter of ribs, he couldn't help but forget his troubles for a moment. The tantalizing aroma made his mouth water, and he was eager to dig in.

"Can I get you anything else?" she asked, scanning the area to see if anyone needed her.

"Not at all, everything's perfect. Thanks," he assured the flustered server, who blushed.

Richard's attention was entirely on the scrumptious ribs before him. He didn't care that she'd forgotten his coleslaw or that she brought him a sweet tea rather than the cola he'd ordered. Now that his favorite dish sat in front of him, he didn't want another interruption until he licked the bones clean. The tantalizing meat coated in the savory sauce called to him, and he couldn't wait to savor every bite.

The waitress heaved a sigh of relief as she hurried over to a nearby table where three mischievous toddlers had just knocked over a pitcher of water. Their gleeful laughter turned into bawling howls as their parents scolded them, and the commotion quickly disrupted the peaceful ambiance of the outdoor dining area.

The mom jumped up, knocking her chair backward as the water soaked through her entire front. She scolded the waitress for being too slow in getting her a dry towel. The relative peacefulness of the outdoor dining fled in an instant of chaos.

Richard couldn't help but chuckle inwardly at the scene. "Well, at least it's a warm afternoon," he thought, imagining that a cool dousing wouldn't be all that bad at the moment.

As he tried to refocus on his own table, his phone continued to ping incessantly with messages from his executive assistant, Brandy. Richard couldn't help but be annoyed at the frivolous interruptions. "Can't I have a lunch hour all to myself?" he grumbled, swiping the screen to see what urgent matter required twenty-three text messages in a mere ten minutes.

"You have got to be kidding me," Richard muttered in disbelief. One message after another extolled the virtues of Brandy's latest fling. Only this time, the guy managed to find the one thing Brandy found irresistible. Sailing. Unbelievably, she accepted his invitation to sail around the world and already left. "I guess today can get worse."

Richard ran his fingers through his slightly disheveled hair, wincing at the sweaty strands. Having left the gym in haste, he hadn't bothered to shower or change his clothes. In his current state, nobody would give him a second glance, unlike when he usually donned his impeccable custom-tailored Alexander Amosu Vanquish suits.

Slamming his phone down onto the table, Richard was determined to push all thoughts of Brandy, Lillith, and his father's incessant advice out of his mind. Right now, he needed to focus on filling his empty stomach. The relief of Brandy leaving, despite the inconvenience, rushed through him. At least he wouldn't have to deal with her drama and find a way to fire her without legal repercussions.

With a sigh, he realized he'd have to ask one of his sales team members to step in for Brandy until he found a replacement.

He preferred a lean staff, but this sudden departure left him in a bind. As much as his father criticized his small team, Richard remained steadfast in his decision. Maxwell Kingston might have a successful CPA firm, but he didn't understand the complexities of running an international luxury airplane manufacturing company like Kingston Air.

His father's constant comparisons to his brother's success in the family business had become tiresome. Richard was determined to prove himself, to show that he could make his own mark in the world. He had no desire to be stuck behind a desk pushing papers eighty hours a week for overly-entitled customers; he wanted to soar, quite literally. Building the world's most exclusive jets was his passion, and he relished the challenge.

Richard didn't need his father's advice on how to run his company or who he should marry. He was determined to make it on his own terms, even if it meant facing constant comparisons and criticism. He'd prove to his family, especially his father and brother, that he could achieve greatness in his own way. And the best part? He'd wake up every day excited to go to work, knowing he was living his dream.

Lifting the first rib to his mouth, Richard's taste buds erupted in delight as he savored the smoky, succulent flavor. All thoughts of discord and comparison fled from his thoughts as he single-mindedly consumed his lunch. The generous amount of sauce used by the pitmaster made him thank his lucky stars that he was still dressed in his gym clothes, sparing him the hassle of expensive dry-cleaning.

Yet, as he relished the meal, his mind couldn't help but wander back to the laundry that Brandy was supposed to have taken care of. He bet she hadn't even left the pick-up slip for him to find. The thought of dealing with the mundane details that Brandy had usually handled grated on his nerves.

Just then, a commotion down the block caught his attention, providing a welcome distraction. His dark thoughts vanished as he watched a pack of dogs excitedly pulling a young lady behind them. He couldn't help but be amused by the scene, and he sat back to enjoy the show, wiping the sticky sauce from his fingers with the oversized napkin.

Her blonde ponytail swayed back and forth as she turned to speak with the fluffy little dog falling behind the rest of the larger ones leading the charge down the sidewalk. It was hard to believe such a small-framed woman could maintain control, limited as it was, yet the dogs seemed content with the pace she set.

Her face lit up with joy as she interacted with the dogs, and it was evident she loved her job. Richard couldn't help but be captivated by her. The woman wore a uniform with the name of a dog-walking service emblazoned in bold pink letters outlined in black.

As he continued to watch her, thoroughly entertained, he failed to notice the rottweiler that had approached him. The large dog's paws landed on his chest, and before he knew it, its massive tongue was giving him an unexpected slobbery greeting. Richard's surprise was evident, and the unexpected encounter left him momentarily stunned.

"Down! Reba! No!" the woman called out, her eyebrows lowering, and her bottom lip instantly got caught up between her teeth as she pulled the dog away from him. "I'm so sorry! I can pay for dry cleaning. Please, sir. I'm so sorry. I don't know what got into Reba. She's normally so shy and reserved."

As Richard wiped the dog slobber and streaks of barbecue sauce off his cheek, he couldn't help but chuckle at the woman's apologetic expression. "No need to worry. Reba seems to have a taste for the rib sauce here," he quipped with a grin, holding up the napkin as evidence of the canine's culinary preferences. "No harm done."

The dogs continued to surround them, and Reba, undeterred by the scolding, managed to snatch a leftover bone from Richard's plate.

"Reba! No!" Anne-Marie's attempts to retrieve it were thwarted by the leashes and the other dogs' playful antics. "Oh, my gosh. I'm so going to get fired for this! I'm so sorry, sir."

"I promise it's fine," Richard reassured her, amused by the chaos unfolding before him. "I was finished anyway, and that bone only had a little sauce left on it. It won't hurt her to gnaw on it."

Standing up, he introduced himself, "I'm Rich, by the way," though he belatedly realized his fingers were still sticky with sauce.

Without any hesitation, she shook his hand firmly, her lips pulling back politely while her eyes betrayed her confusion and concern. "I'm Anne-Marie." She quickly scolded Reba again, who seemed unperturbed and continued to gnaw on the bone. "I can't believe you, Reba. That was terrible manners."

The dog moved until she was in the shadow of the table, the bone nestled between her front paws. She didn't even look up from her contented bone gnawing with the sides of her back teeth.

As Richard pondered his chance encounter with Anne-Marie, a light bulb of opportunity flickered in his mind. "Do you believe in fate?" he asked suddenly, hoping to convey his genuine interest.

"What? You're not hitting on me right now, are you?"

"No!" He held up his hands as if to ward her off and realized how rude that gesture seemed. The expression transforming her face confirmed he had offended her. "Sorry, I'd like to, but that's not what I meant at all. Ugh. This isn't coming out right. Let me start over." He closed his eyes and took a deep breath.

With composure regained, he continued, "You mentioned needing this job, and I just happen to know of a really good place to work that's hiring. Would you be interested?"

Anne-Marie's eyes narrowed, and her head cocked to the side. "You're not one of those creepy photographers, are you?"

Richard couldn't help but laugh. Where did she come up with this stuff? "No. Not at all. Have you ever heard of Kingston Air?"

"No. I'm not from around here. I just moved to town."

"Oh, no bother. Here," Richard said with enthusiasm, reaching into his gym bag to retrieve a business card. He handed it to her, adding, "The executive assistant just quit today, and we're in desperate need of a replacement. If you're interested, give this number a call, and we can arrange an interview."

Though her fingers hovered close to the card, she hesitated, expressing doubt about her qualifications. "I don't have any office experience. I doubt I'd qualify."

With a determined look, Richard pressed the business card into Anne-Marie's hand, urging her to seize the opportunity. "Trust me; the last girl wasn't qualified either, but she managed just fine. You'll do great," he reassured her, a glint of excitement in his eyes.

He then realized he was running late and had to get back to work. He grabbed his bag and slung it over his shoulder. "I don't mean to be rude, but I've got to run," he explained apologetically. "Don't wait too long to call. This could be your chance for something amazing."

As he hurried away, he almost stumbled over a playful dog darting in front of him. Collecting himself, he made his way to where his Phantom was parked. Richard was glad that Anne-Marie didn't witness him getting into his fancy car; he didn't want to overwhelm her.

Nonetheless, he couldn't shake off the feeling that he needed to do more to encourage her. Maybe revealing that he owned Kingston Air would help break down any barriers. He decided that if he didn't hear from her by the end of the next business day, he'd make a discreet inquiry at the dog-walking shop to find a way to reach her again.

If you enjoyed this sample, Plane Love is available now.

GET MY FREE BOOK NOW

To let others know how much you enjoyed this book, please leave a review at your favorite retailer.

To keep updated on upcoming books, visit www.amyproebstel.com.

Receive a FREE prequel story,

A Billionaire's Patent for Love

by signing up for Amy Proebstel's newsletter.

You can also follow Amy Proebstel on Facebook at www.facebook.com/ATwistOnReality.

About the Author

Amy is a *USA Today* bestselling author who writes a sweet romance and young adult medical romance.

When she's not busy writing about endearing heroes, scheming villains, and Lone Star love stories, she spends her time binge-watching Hallmark movies, taking her husband and daughter flying (but not in the jets her billionaire's fly), playing with her Pomeranian and Pomskies, and cats, or reading.

A.B. Proebstel is the sweet romance pen name for Amy Proebstel, who also writes progression fantasy, epic dragon fantasy, and paranormal romance books that add a little magic to the world.

Please sign up for Amy's fantasy or romance newsletters on

her website at www.AmyProebstel.com or click Follow on her bio to get notices and updates when she releases new books!

- Get a bonus scene from A Cowboy's Recipe for Romance: https://geni.us/B1-ACRFR-Bonus

- Join her mailing list: https://geni.us/CleanRomance

- Join her Facebook group: facebook.com/ATwistOnReality

- Visit her website: amyproebstel.com

- Follow her on X: https://geni.us/Amy-T

- Follow her on Instagram: instagram.com/amyproebstel

She loves hearing from her readers.

Also By

Amy Proebstel

Billionaire's Bet, A Sweet Romance Series

Sweet Creek Ranch, A Sweet Romance Series

Wolf Shifters of Catskill County, A Clean Fated Mate Shifter Series

The Chosen, A Fantasy & Magic Adventure Series

Dragon's Magic: An Epic Dragon Fantasy Series

The Rift in Our Reality, A Sweet Young Adult Medical Romance

9 781946 292360